The Monster Hunter's Manual

Book 1: Skeletons and Traps

The Monster Hunter's Manual

Book 1: Skeletons and Traps

Jessica Penot

OUR STREET
BOOKS

Winchester, UK
Washington, USA

First published by Our Street Books, 2014
Our Street Books is an imprint of John Hunt Publishing Ltd., Laurel House, Station Approach,
Alresford, Hants, SO24 9JH, UK
office1@jhpbooks.net
www.johnhuntpublishing.com
www.ourstreet-books.com

For distributor details and how to order please visit the 'Ordering' section on our website.

Text copyright: Jessica Penot 2012

ISBN: 978 1 78099 933 3

A CIP catalogue record for this book is available from the British Library.

Design: Stuart Davies

Illustrations and cover design: Irina Grabarnik

Printed and bound by CPI Group (UK) Ltd, Croydon, CR0 4YY

We operate a distinctive and ethical publishing philosophy in all
areas of our business, from our global network of authors to
production and worldwide distribution.

CONTENTS

Acknowledgements

This book was the vision of my two sons, Gabriel and Xander. Without their unique imagination and creativity, this book would have never been written. Their ideas find breath on the pages of this book. I thank them a thousand times for helping me write this. I would also like to thank my husband who puts up with me wasting all my time writing books and daydreaming.

Chapter 1

The Broken Castle

My mom used to say that all adventures begin with a journey. My mom used to say all kinds of stuff. She liked to take us places and tell us about everything. She took us to Paris once, and told us stories as we walked through the Louvre. She told us stories about kings, queens and the secret magic that all old cities were built on. I wish I had listened better. Now, I can't remember her words. I can only remember the feelings and the sense that the world was older than time and that magic tied it together.

My brother sat up as the plane touched down. He hadn't said anything to me for the entire trip. In fact, Alex and I hadn't talked much at all since the funeral. I suppose we thought that if we didn't say anything, then none of it would be real. If we didn't say our parents were dead, they might show up at any minute and take us home.

Alex and I waited while everyone else got off the plane. We weren't in any hurry. We weren't going any place we wanted to be. The people around us talked and I could get an idea of what they were feeling, but I didn't understand what anyone was saying. I had never learned French. My dad had tried to teach me. He had sat with me going over lesson after lesson and I had stared off into space thinking about video games or movies.

Finally, the plane cleared and I grabbed my stuff. Alex dragged his feet and his backpack down the aisle of the plane. I poked him in the ribs and told him to move faster and every time I poked him he whined, "Stop."

If all adventures began with a journey, ours had certainly begun. I never wanted to see an airplane again. It had taken us three airplane rides to get to Poitiers and I felt completely lost. When we got off this airplane, I felt even more lost. All the signs were in French and no one spoke any English. We wandered this way and that until we found our way to customs. An angry looking guard who barked at us in French, stamped our passports, and we collected our bags.

I hadn't seen Aunt Perrine in over three years. She hadn't been anyone's favorite aunt. My dad always said she lived too far away to visit when we went to France. Everyone else came up to see us in Brittany when we visited, but Aunt Perrine said she didn't like driving and that it was too far.

"Lazy old bag," my mother had complained. "What else does she have to do? It's not like she works. She could come see her nephews. What does she do all day? Knit?"

As we exited the baggage claim, I thought that maybe Aunt Perrine did knit all day. She was wearing an old green sweater that looked like she had made it herself and she had another sweater over it. She had a knitted scarf and even her green, misshapen hat appeared to be made by her.

Aunt Perrine smiled broadly at us and ran towards us. Alex's eyes widened a little in terror as she kissed him on each cheek and exclaimed, "Oh, les enfants! C'estdomage!" And then in English, "Poor little babies!"

She backed away from Alex, leaving him disheveled and covered in red lipstick before she turned to me. "Gabriel," she said with a horrible French accent. "Oh la la, look how big?" And she kissed my cheeks with equal gusto.

I smiled at Aunt Perrine and she took my hand. "Come now," she said and she dragged me away from the airport and into the parking lot where her miniature car sat in the shadows.

Alex grimaced and whispered in my ear, "Can we fit in that car?"

I don't think he was joking. For a minute, as I shoved our suitcases in the trunk of the car, I thought there was no way we would all fit, but we managed to all pile in and Aunt Perrine smiled brightly as she tuned the radio on.

The music was terrible. It was like country music, in French, but Aunt Perrine sang along to every word of the song.

It was a long drive with no stoplights. Instead of the stoplights, the roads had a bunch of circles that you spun around in. Alex and I sat quietly as Aunt Perrine drove and sang.

We watched the French countryside as we might have watched an alien landscape. Everything was so old and so different. Old houses, old churches, even the light seemed old and Aunt Perrine looked like she was the oldest thing of all. The journey was long and it was made longer still by the knowledge that we would never go home again.

We drove through long vineyards and sunflower fields until we came to a tiny town with roads so narrow, even Aunt Perrine's tiny car scraped the sides of the medieval houses as we drove through the road. The village was drawn tightly together and all the houses touched. They were made with old mortar, and even though the Middle Ages had ended five hundred years ago, I thought that maybe I had stepped backwards and fell into them.

Finally, Aunt Perrine took a hard right and the car fought its way up a steep hill and over a drawbridge into the gates of a decaying castle. Inside the walls of the castle, there was a crumbling stone church with demons and gargoyles engraved on the outside. The church was attached to a long wall that rose up into large, half-fallen towers and half a keep. On the other side of the wall, there were little houses built directly into the fortress wall. There were cats everywhere. They sat on the old walls and in the doorway to the church. They reclined lazily and watched us with sleepy eyes.

"Zey used to be for zee servants," Aunt Perrine explained. She pointed to the houses built into the walls. "Do I say zis right?"

I nodded.

"So, zis is us," she said and stopped the car.

Aunt Perrine went to close the castle gate and Alex and I were left staring upward at our new home.

"Why did Mom and Dad do this?" Alex asked suddenly.

"What?" I answered.

"Why didn't they leave us with someone at home? Why didn't they have plans? I hate this place. I hate this country and I hate this castle."

I didn't know what to do so I put my hand on his shoulder. Alex was only seventeen months younger than me, but he was as tall as me and twice as irritable. Sometimes people even thought we were twins. We both had the same dirty, blond hair and bright blue eyes. We both had similar features. Mom even used to try to dress us alike. But Alex and I were as different as steam and snow. I was neat and he was messy. I liked to read and play video games inside and he always wanted to be outside playing with friends or mucking around in the mud. He was loud and I was quiet.

Alex pushed my hand off his shoulder and stalked off in the direction of the castle keep. I realized, sadly, that my birthday was only a week away. I'd be twelve. Mom would have baked me a cake and Dad would've taken us camping.

"What do you zink?" Aunt Perrine asked.

"It's creepy," I answered coldly.

"Oh, yes. And it is very 'aunted." Aunt Perrine winked.

My mouth fell open. "Haunted?"

"Yes, yes," she said.

"Haunted?"

"Yes. Ghosts and monsters and such." She said it happily as if she was talking about a pie she had made for us.

"I don't believe in any of those things."

"Oh, well. Give it time." She opened the trunk of the car.

The servant's quarters had been remodeled into a cozy little home. There was a living room, dining room, and kitchen. The kitchen had a massive medieval fireplace and the floors felt so cold that the cold spread upwards. Aunt Perrine had furnished her home with antiques and covered everything in pink roses and lace doilies.

Her bedroom was downstairs and the stone walls of the room were covered in pictures of kittens and cats saying cute things in French. In the middle of the house, a long, spiral staircase, carried us upstairs to four rooms that had been converted to bedrooms and a bathroom. Up even further, above the heavy brown beams that supported the old structure, were a loft and an attic.

"Don't go up zere," Aunt Perrine said as we past the stairs up to the loft. "Zis is very, very 'aunted."

I opened the door to my room. It was clean and neat. A large, lazy gray cat was sitting on my bed purring loudly and the walls had been hung with large tapestries to keep the cold out. There was a weird rug on the ground that looked like it was bearskin, but it had three eyes and a smashed face. Its fur was purple and matted.

"You like?" Aunt Perrine asked.

"I guess," I answered.

Aunt Perrine walked over to the cat and petted her. The cat leaned into her hand and purred even more loudly. "Zis is Bastet," she said. "She is zee queen of zee cats. She sleeps in 'ere wiz you. You be good to 'er."

"OK." I petted the cat's soft fur.

Alex's room was a little smaller than mine and the sheep skin rug on the floor wasn't even half as interesting as the rug in my room, but the window in his room looked out on the village bellow and had a cool, airplane comforter on the bed.

"Your mamman said zat you like planes, Alex? No?"

Alex nodded.

"Now you boys get settled and zen come down for gateau...cake."

We both agreed and when she left we fell on our beds like logs. We were so tired we could hardly stand. Alex began to cry softly and Bastet came and sat on his belly. He stroked her fur and wept. "I wanna go home."

"Me too."

"This place is creepy."

"It's just old."

"Everything here is weird."

I shrugged my shoulders. "It's France."

Alex brushed the tears from his eyes and gave a great sniff. "I don't like it."

"Well, it doesn't matter. We're stuck here."

He wiped his nose on his hand in response.

"That's gross, you're disgusting."

"Well, you smell," he retorted.

"Well at least my arm isn't covered in snot," I responded.

Alex stuck his tongue out at me and rolled off the bed. He swung the door wide open and ran into the hall.

"What're you doing?" I asked.

Alex frowned. "I'm going upstairs."

"Aunt Perrine told you not to do that."

"I don't care. Why should I care? I want to see what that crazy, old lady is hiding up there!"

"You're going to get us both in trouble."

"I don't care." Alex ran up the spiral stairs and they groaned angrily with each step he took. He stopped at the top and looked down at me.

"You better not!" I yelled.

Alex looked up defiantly and disappeared into the darkness. I waited. I thought he would come back and tell me there was nothing up there, but some old French books and old lady stuff, but the silence only seemed to grow.

"Alex!"

There was no answer. I moved towards the stairs and bent my neck so I could see into the loft, but the lights were off and I couldn't see through the darkness.

"Alex!" I yelled again. "Get down here or I'm telling on you!"

Still there was no noise. I stepped onto the stairs. They whined more loudly with each step I took. I crept to the top and took a large step onto the floor of the loft. It took a few minutes for my eyes to adjust to the dark. I could just make out shapes in the shadows. There were boxes and the outlines of what looked like furniture, but there was no Alex. My heart raced a little. I could still hear Aunt Perrine saying it was a very haunted in the loft. I stumbled over something in the darkness and then something big hit me in the face.

I panicked as whatever it was fell off my face and down my shirt. I started yelling and jumping up and down in a silly attempt to remove whatever it was. I could feel legs and cold feet on my stomach.

I screamed and fell backwards hitting my head on the banister. The pain was sharp and when I stood back up a large plastic spider fell out of my shirt and onto the floor. Alex jumped out of the darkness and laughed and then ran down the stairs.

"I'm going to kill you!" I crushed the plastic spider with the ball of my foot and followed him down stairs. I caught up with him in the hall and tackled him. He fell onto the floor and started yelling as I jumped on top of him. I punched at him as hard as I could and he screamed out.

"I hate you!" Alex wailed as he covered his face. "You don't even care that Mom and Dad are dead. You like it here in this creepy, old place!"

I stopped hitting him and looked at his tear stained face. "That's not true," I said. "Just 'cause I don't mope around all the time and cry like a baby doesn't meant I don't care."

"Why'd they leave us?" Alex asked, still weeping.

"Sometimes people just die. I don't think they meant to

leave us."

Alex pushed me again and I fell off him. I let him run into his room and close the door. I shook my head and dusted myself off. For a minute, I just sat on the floor. I wasn't sure what to do, but I finally decided to just go to bed. I walked down to the kitchen, where Aunt Perrine sat with a cup of tea and some kind of pastry. It looked good, but it wasn't cake. "I'm going to bed," I told her.

"You 'ave zee gateau," she said. "You will feel better."

I sat down beside her at the table. She had put on another sweater over the other ones. She looked like a big, overstuffed pillow. She smiled. "You eat zee cake."

"My brother won't come down."

"He will come down." Aunt Perrine's voice was pleasant.

I looked down at the tablecloth. It was covered in pictures of fluffy kittens playing with balls of string. I nodded and ate the pastry. It was good, a creamy mixture of chocolate and almond that melted in my mouth before I had chewed the first bite. When I ate it, I felt warm, from the tips of my toes up to my nose. The warmth spread over me, I took another bite and I felt strangely happy. By the time I was done with the cake, I felt peaceful and ready for bed. Aunt Perrine washed the chocolate off my face as if I was a baby, and I smiled dumbly up at her.

"Now you sleep," she said.

I went upstairs to my bedroom and crawled into bed. I meant to sleep. I wanted to listen to her. She was a sweet, old lady. But the floors moaned and the wind blew and the castle hid shadows and secrets. Bastet sat at the foot of my bed purring so loudly it sounded like a lawnmower in the silence of the night.

I got out of bed and sat up at the window looking out at the courtyard. The castle looked haunting in the moonlight. Nothing moved except the cats that crept in and out of the shadows.

I watched the darkness, imagining how the castle might have been years ago, and my eyes grew heavy until sleep almost took me, but then a small light cut through the darkness. I sat up and squinted. I could see Aunt Perrine walking toward the old keep in the dark. She was wearing her horrible, knitted bathrobe and cap, and she had a book in her hand.

She walked across the courtyard and into the keep and shut the door behind her. A light appeared in the window of the old keep. I could almost see her, but I couldn't imagine what she was doing. I opened my window and tried to listen. I leaned out. I thought I heard singing. I waited, but Aunt Perrine stayed in the keep and I gave in to my exhaustion and climbed back into bed.

Chapter 2

The Very Haunted Attic

The sun hadn't risen when Alex came running into my room and jumped into bed with me. He crammed himself into my tiny bed and pushed his cold feet up against me.

"Get out!" I complained. "Your feet are cold."

"There's a ghost upstairs."

"I'm not falling for it a second time."

"You gotta believe me. There's something upstairs!"

"Get out!" I yelled and pushed him onto the ground.

Alex stood back up. He didn't try to get back in bed with me, but stood beside the bed shivering. I could see his face in the moonlight and he was white as a sheet. I could tell he was really afraid so I sat up and looked around. From my window I could see the courtyard and the crumbling keep. The wind was blowing and the trees bent in the wind. There was a full moon.

"OK," I said. "So, let's check it out."

I rifled around in my suitcase until I found a flashlight and turned it on. I pulled my robe on and opened the door to my room. Alex hugged my side. There was a large thud from the room above us and I dropped my flashlight. Alex grabbed my arm.

"It's probably a mouse or something," I decided.

I bent over to pick up my flashlight and there was another thud, a bang and a large clanging noise. My hand shook making the light dance on the ground in front of me. I shone the light into the empty hall. Everything was still and quiet. Moonlight shone in from the open window and spilled out onto the floor. There was another bang, but this time it was louder.

"It's a big rat," I whispered.

The banging stopped and then there were voices – whispering in tones that didn't seem human. The voices were speaking in French, and even if it had been English, we wouldn't have understood them. The male voices were getting louder, as if they were fighting.

"They are big, talking rats," I said stupidly.

Something screamed and there was another bang. Alex ran and I froze. I stood with my feet planted on the floor clutching my flashlight like a sword. There was another bang and a wail. I dropped the flashlight again, but this time it broke as it hit the floor. The batteries scattered across the old wood and darkness swallowed the room. Alex ran towards my bed and pulled the covers up over his head. I stood rooted to the ground, unable to move.

The thuds stopped and I closed my eyes trying to think of some explanation for the noise. Bang! The crash was so loud that the light fixture above me shook. I ran to the door, closed it, and twisted the lock. I leaned against the thick wooden door, holding it shut. There was another thud and I jumped in bed next to my brother. I pulled the covers over my head and lay perfectly still staring at him.

"I told you. There are ghosts up there," Alex said.

I could still hear Aunt Perrine saying it was a very haunted attic. "I don't believe in ghosts."

Alex kept his voice low. "Then why are you shaking?"

"Because they might be burglars."

"Right. They climbed the castle walls to break into an attic? Or did they break down the drawbridge?"

"Maybe." I frowned.

"You are so stupid," Alex hissed.

"At least I don't believe in ghosts like a baby."

There was another thud and then a strange cracking noise, Alex and I both looked up. Alex grabbed my hand

and despite ourselves, we huddled up under the covers together to wait for dawn.

The light peeked in the window of my room dispelling the fear of the long night. Alex and I had fallen asleep but we hadn't slept long. We both sat up and pulled the covers down. There were birds singing in the distance. In the bright light of morning, our fear seemed a little silly.

We could hear Aunt Perrine singing down stairs so we followed the sound of her voice down into the kitchen. Aunt Perrine was already dressed for the day and sitting at the table with a tiny glass of coffee and a croissant. She smiled broadly, as always.

"There's ghosts in the attic!" Alex yelled.

"Bien sur," she said. "Of course. I say to you, zis attic is very 'aunted, no?"

"It may have been burglars," I added.

Aunt Perrine laughed. "Zis castle stood against ze armies of ze English when zey come. It stand against ze Vikings. You zink burglars can come in? No. N'est pas possible!"

"So they were ghosts!" Alex exclaimed.

"Yes, I say so," Aunt Perrine said.

Alex shook fearfully. "What can we do?"

"Nozing. You do nozing. Zey won't 'urt you."

"But..."

"No buts," she said. "Would you like a croissant?"

We both sat down and she gave us each a croissant and hot chocolate. Aunt Perrine hummed as she made it, slowly boiling the milk and pouring it over the chocolate. She smiled at us as she set the cups down. The windows were open and the sunshine poured in through the lace curtains and onto the floor. Despite everything that happened, both Alex and I were filled with a sudden urge to explore. It was a beautiful day and we were in a fascinating place.

Everything else could be easily forgotten.

We both shoved the croissant into our mouths and slurped our hot chocolate down as fast as we could.

"Can we go outside?" I asked with a mouth full of croissant.

Aunt Perrine laughed again. "You come to zee store wiz me and zen you go. I don't know what boyz eat."

Alex's little smile faded and he sat back down. We both shuffled back upstairs and put on our clothes. Alex took his time and hung out of his bedroom window watching the people running to and fro in the medieval village below us. It was a busy village and people were sitting outside in a café drinking coffee. Other people ran down the street with baguettes in their hands. Alex scowled as he watched the pretty scene.

"I don't wanna go to the store," Alex whined.

"Me either," I said.

There was another thump from upstairs and Alex jumped up angrily. He deliberately stomped across the floor and back to the winding staircase. "I don't care about ghosts either," he yelled. "You hear me ghosts! I'm coming up!" He ran up the stairs and I followed him. We burst into the loft and switched on the lights.

The lamps flickered and then a pale glow spread over the loft. It was dirty and dusty, but quiet. Alex grabbed my hand and pulled me in with him. He was shaking a little. The loft looked like someone's bedroom. There were was an old bed on one side of the room and a couple of chests. There were books spread out over the floor.

I picked one up and read the title, "A Skeleton's Guide to Broken Bones."

I dropped the book and shrugged. There were several bottles in the corner and Alex picked one up and read the label, *"Diet Blood."*

"Diet Blood?" I asked.

"It's *Sans Sucre*," Alex read the rest of the label. "Whatever that means." He dropped the bottle on the floor and it made an ominous clanking noise. He kicked the bottle as it hit the floor and it rolled under the bed.

Alex opened the chest while I studied the bookshelf. It was stacked high with old books. I picked one up and looked at the pictures. It showed an army of skeletons fighting a horrible monster. I couldn't read the text. It was all in French. I turned the page. There was another picture that showed some kind of sorceress or witch casting a spell on the monster. I slid the book in pocket of my bathrobe and looked at the rest of the things on the shelf.

There were lots of games. Checkers, Life, and Sorry, were all stacked up haphazardly on the shelf. There was a piece of old chewing gum stuck to the bottom of one shelf.

Alex continued rifling through the chest and pulled out a stack of old clothes. He threw them on the floor and stared at them.

"They're all kid's clothes," he said. "Do you think Aunt Perrine had kids?"

I shrugged.

There were posters on the walls with pictures from old monster movies. "Maybe it's a joke," I said.

"Let's see what's in the attic." Alex pushed open the door to the attic. A wave of hot air came out. There were no lights but we looked in. There were boxes and a coffin. "There's a coffin!"

"Maybe a vampire lives up here," I said sarcastically.

"Yeah, right," Alex answered. "Maybe Aunt Perrine keeps her dead husband up here."

"She's not *that* crazy."

Alex smiled and made a funny face and did a hand motion around his head to indicate that she was crazy.

"She's crazy." He did a little dance.

I laughed.

"I save it for when I die," Aunt Perrine said. Alex and I jumped. Aunt Perrine had appeared out of nowhere. Alex screamed like a little girl and I fell backwards.

"I save it for when I die," she said again.

"What?" I asked.

"Zee coffin. I buy it on sale."

"Oh," I said.

"I like to shop zee sales."

"Oh," I said again.

"Come on. Time to go to zee store."

Aunt Perrine scuffled down the stairs in her strange slippers leaving Alex and me staring after her with our mouths slightly agape. I closed the door to the attic and Alex looked at me. "She's crazy. Isn't she?"

I didn't know what to say, so I shrugged and followed her down the stairs. Alex caught up with me and tugged at my shoulder. "You don't think she's crazy?" he demanded.

"I don't know. I wish I did. I know we are stuck here, so we might as well make the best of it instead of sulking around and complaining."

Alex pushed me. "I'm not doing that."

"Yes, you are." I pushed him back.

"Yeah. Well maybe you should complain too. It's like Mom and Dad didn't even die. You don't even care that they're dead."

"Shut your stupid mouth," I said and punched him in the shoulder.

Alex kicked me in the shin and ran down the stairs after Aunt Perrine. My face flushed with anger. What did Alex know? Just because I didn't mope around and cry like a baby didn't mean I didn't care. He ran around the kitchen table and out the front door into the fortress courtyard.

I followed. In the sunlight, it was pretty. Wild roses crept up the walls and soft grass covered the ground. Cats sat lazily basking in the sunshine. Aunt Perrine was raising the castle gate and Alex was running towards her.

I knew what he was thinking. He was thinking I wouldn't hit him in front of her, but he was stupid. I tackled Alex and sat on top of him hitting him.

"You take it back!" I wailed.

Aunt Perrine lifted me off. She was strong for an old lady. I fell back into the dirt. The tears burned in my eyes.

Aunt Perrine sat down in the dirt next to us and put her hand on each of ours. "Boyz," she said softly. "It will be all right. You will see. You 'ave strong 'earts. You are fighters and zee world needs fighters."

Aunt Perrine embraced us both, and we leaned into her. "Bad zings 'appen," she said. "Terrible zings, but there is always light at the end. You vill see."

Alex and I nodded.

"Now you be nice."

We both nodded again.

"So now we go to zee store."

She got up and we both followed her into her tiny car. She sang all the way to the store. The castle was located in a tiny village, called Chateau Larcher, just like the castle. There was no grocery store in the village, so we had to drive all the way back into the city. It was a long ride.

The grocery store, or supermarche, was big and crowded. At first, it almost looked like a store at home, until you looked at the labels. Alex hung behind Aunt Perrine with a scowl and the occasional look of disgust when he saw something weird.

Everything was different, even the soda – Orangina? The snacks were different too – Mininizza's? I picked up the package. They were small pizza like crackers. They looked good. I put them down and chased after Aunt Perrine. I caught up with her at the meat aisle. It was just disgusting. There were whole birds with their heads and feet still attached. Every organ that could be taken out of an animal was neatly packaged and labeled.

Alex snickered when we passed an entire section of brains. He pointed and called out to me.

"Brains!" he yelled. "They have brains!"

Aunt Perrine turned the cart around and smiled. "Oh zanks you, Alex," she said. "I almost forget."

She pulled the cart up alongside the brain section and filled it up. Cow brains. Sheep brains. Goose brains. She took every brain there was and smiled while she did it. And then she looked at us. "So, now what do you boyz want?"

We picked out the most familiar foods we could find, breakfast cereal, fruit and chips. They had something that looked like hotdogs. The peanut butter had some kind of oil floating on top, so we avoided that. We got what we could, and when Aunt Perrine went to pay, Alex looked at me with genuine concern.

"She isn't going to feed us brains every night, is she?"

I shrugged.

"I'm not eating brains," Alex said.

I shrugged again.

"You aren't going to eat brains, are you?"

"I don't know," I answered. "Dad said they were good. Dad used to eat them when we visited Nannan."

"You are just as crazy as Aunt Perrine."

I shrugged again. I didn't care. I just couldn't wait to get back to the castle and explore.

Chapter 3

The Ghost of the Keep

My mom used to drag us through Paris and she never got tired. She would pull us through the underworld of the subways, where the trains never slept and had complained as she walked, "Sometimes there's just too much to see." She had then smiled and winked at me and leaned down and whispered in my ear, "This place is magic you know."

"The subway?" I had asked.

"Yes," she had said. "These tunnels go on forever and deep beneath the earth there are magic creatures that live forever."

I remember being a little scared then. "Are they bad?"

"No," my mother had answered. "They saved your father once."

"Really?"

"Really." She had said it in the way she said lots of things. I had never been sure if she was just telling a story or if she really meant it.

I thought about it as I started out into the castle. There was too much to see. Alex ran ahead of me. "Come on," he shouted.

I followed him up the first tower of the broken castle. The old wooden door whined as it opened, and Alex ran up the long, spiral stairs, to the top of the tower. From the top, you could see the entire village and the countryside beyond it.

Alex laughed. "I bet knights used to stand guard up here and shoot people with their arrows. Don't you think?"

"It was probably just a watchtower," I answered.

"You are such a killjoy, sometimes." He ran down the

stairs and up to the top of the castle gate. There were two towers on either side of it The towers had tiny slit windows. The area just on top of the gate had slit windows too. Alex smiled. "Archers could stand here and fire out on the people who were attacking them!" He pretended to draw his bow and fire out onto the imaginary armies beneath us.

I looked out of the hole at the village and tried to imagine what it must have been like. I tried to imagine armies of knights in shining armor moving up the hill towards us with swords drawn.

"This is awesome!" Alex declared. He ran to the next tower. "Why didn't we come here before?"

"Dad and Aunt Perrine didn't get along," I said.

"Why not?"

"I don't know. They had some kind of fight when we were both little. Mom always wanted them to work it out, but Dad wouldn't. Mom always tried to talk to Aunt Perrine, but Dad got so upset she just let it go."

"What did they fight about?"

"I don't know. You'd have to ask Aunt Perrine."

"No way! She's crazy," he said.

I joined Alex and pretended to draw my bow and fire at the oncoming hoards of knights. Alex drew his sword and faced me. "You won't take this castle."

"Your pitiful army won't stop us," I replied and we pretended to fight along the castle walls. We clashed invisible swords for a while and then we ran down the stairs and back out into the courtyard. The sun spilled over the half-broken walls and onto the sweet, summer grass, and we ran in and out of broken remains of what was once some kind of barn. We jumped on the walls fighting all the way and then ran into the remains of the castle keep. An old door led to more stairs, which in turn led to a small room by a window. The small room was all that was left of the keep. The rest of it had crumbled.

We stood in the room and looked at the broken timbers from the roof and the remains of moldy tapestries. Alex kicked the beams and looked around.

I thought the room must have been beautiful once. There was an old bed with large, claw feet. There were cherubs carved on the headboard and bed curtains still hung in tattered disrepair from the canopy. There was a broken mirror and an old chest. There were elaborate chairs engraved with angels and saints. Dull light streamed in from one small, barred window, making the dust in the room seem even thicker. All of this beauty sat as if it hadn't been touched for a thousand years.

"I bet this is where they kept the prisoners," he said.

"I don't think so."

"This is the prison," he asserted.

"Why would they have tapestries in a prison?"

"I don't know," Alex said. "Why would they have bars on the windows if it wasn't a prison?"

"Maybe to keep people out?"

"I think it's a prison," Alex said again.

He picked up an old piece of wood and pretended it was a sword. He parried and thrust and I watched him. Something moved in the shadows, behind one of the old tapestries. The tapestry fluttered and I moved it aside. There was nothing but stone wall behind it.

"Did you see that?" I asked.

"What?" Something else moved, this time by the edge of a broken bed. It moved behind the bed curtains. The bed curtains were ruined and faded. Time had decayed them, but I could see that they had once been beautiful red velvet, and had been embroidered with tiny flowers.

"This was a bedroom," I whispered to myself.

"It was the room of the Lord's daughter," a small voice answered from the shadows.

Both Alex and I turned. We could see someone hiding behind the remains of a tapestry, but we couldn't see who.

"She was a princess..." The voice was a whisper.

Alex moved towards me and stood slightly behind me with his fake sword drawn.

"What was that?" he whispered in my ear.

I stepped away from him and moved towards the tapestry. "Who are you?" I demanded. "And what are you doing here?"

"What are you doing here?" the small voice responded. It was a girl's voice.

"We live here," I answered.

The girl stepped out of the corner. I could see her. She was pretty and pale. She seemed almost like an angel in the shadows and was the prettiest girl I had ever seen, like a picture from a fairytale. I couldn't see her very well, but she had long blond hair and blue eyes. She wore a long dress that dragged against the dirty floor when she moved. There were jewels braided into her hair. She was probably no more than twelve, but something in the way she stood gave her authority.

"I live here too," she said.

"Really?" Alex asked.

She nodded and stepped into the sunlight. The girl was pale – so pale the sun passed right through her. I think I should have been afraid. Alex jumped a little, but she was so pretty and sweet that there was no way I could be afraid.

"You're a ghost," I said plainly.

"Yes."

"Did you used to live here?"

"I still do," she said.

"I mean, when you were alive?"

"Oh it doesn't matter that I live here because I'm a ghost?" she said.

I could feel myself flushing. I hadn't meant to offend her and my words seemed to be coming out all wrong. "No, that's not what I meant."

She shook her head in disagreement. "Well, that's what you said. This is my room. It's always been my room."

"Well," Alex said. "It's gross and dirty."

"That's because you lack the vision to see it as it really

is," she said.

"I can see fine."

"How does it really look?" I asked.

The girl stepped forward and smiled at me. "Do you want me to show you?"

I nodded. I could hardly breathe. This was like magic. Like real magic. We were in a magic castle!

"Don't let her do it!" Alex yelled. "She'll suck your brains out or something."

"Shut up," I said.

The girl reached out and passed her hand through me. It tingled. I closed my eyes. "You have the gift," she whispered softly.

I opened my eyes and I saw the room as it had once been. I saw a large bed, like a princess's, hung with beautiful fabric. There was a large fireplace in the corner and the walls were covered in tapestries. These were bright and new, showing pictures of unicorns and princesses sitting in tents.

Beneath the tapestries, three pretty young girls sat doing embroidery, little dogs at their feet. The girls talked and laughed as they worked.

I looked out the window and saw the castle. The walls were high and flags decorated with red lions, waved in the wind. The courtyard was crowded with peasants working. There was a man in the corner working in a small enclave. He seemed to be a blacksmith working his craft. Another man was saddling horses and there were a group of women carrying heavy baskets somewhere. Children ran through the courtyard laughing and two men practiced fighting with wooden swords. An older man sat on a stool cleaning something. Everyone was busy.

Just behind the courtyard, the keep stood like it had just been built. The keep was a beautiful home for the lord of the land. Knights practiced their sword fighting on the mound just beyond the castle keep. The sound of their clashing swords rose above the other sounds in the courtyard.

A young boy saddled a horse by the barn and a pair of pretty maidens walked through the castle gates. The church doors were thrown open, and as the bells sounded, people stopped their work and began to walk towards them.

I smiled and the image faded, like a movie fading out. I turned around and everything was as it had been. "It's beautiful," I said.

"I know," she replied.

"I'm Gabriel."

"I'm Eleanor," she said in a crisp, British accent.

"Why don't you speak French?"

"When I lived here," she said. "The English held this part of France. The Great Queen Eleanor, after whom I am named, and Henry II the Plantagenet, ruled all of England and most of France."

I smiled at her. "I didn't know that."

"When the French came and took this castle, it fell and no one bothered to fix it. Your aunt's the only one who's lived here since then."

"Really?"

She nodded.

"You've been here all alone?"

She laughed. "No silly. This place is filled with friends. Why would I stay alone?"

"What friends?"

"Would you like to meet them?" Her grin was mischievous.

"Yes!"

"Don't tell your Aunt Perrine, OK?"

"Of course not."

"Can I come too?" Alex asked from the corner.

Eleanor gave him a mean glare and then smiled and nodded. "I haven't had any other children to play with in forever," she said. She turned and led us out of the keep.

Eleanor almost vanished as she stepped into the courtyard. The sun made her nothing but a whisper of light and we had to squint to see her. She ran and we had to go as fast as we could to keep up with her. We could hear her laughter as she passed under the castle gates and out into the driveway. She took us down a sharp path behind the castle to a cave, which went under the castle. There were bars in front of it, but she raised them so we could pass under. In the darkness of the cave, I could see Eleanor more clearly than ever. She glowed in the dark. I could see her long golden hair tied back in a braid and her long, velvet gown tied at the waist with a jeweled belt.

She was so bright we could see the cave, even in the dark. And it wasn't a cave, it was a tunnel. It was hundreds of tunnels built beneath the castle out of stone. Eleanor laughed and led us into the darkness until we were so far underground we couldn't have found our way out if we tried.

"I don't like this," Alex whined.

I took his hand and smiled at him. "It's going to be OK. This is magic. Just like Mom used to say. Don't you remember?"

"No," he said.

"She used to say that there was magic in all these old places, if we had eyes to see them. She said that there were adventures in every shadow and we should never turn away from an adventure."

"She said that?"

I nodded and Alex smiled. His grip tightened in my

hand and we pushed on, following our phantom friend to a large room filled with an underground garden. It didn't even seem real it was so beautiful. A waterfall poured out of what appeared to be an underground portion of the castle and there were flowers everywhere. I watched Eleanor. She was the prettiest thing in the room and her radiance illuminated everything, bathing it in a warm glow.

She smiled and made a strange cooing sound and two dozen gleaming eyes appeared around us in the darkness.

Eleanor said something in French and more than a dozen, strange fuzzy creatures lumbered out from the shadows. Alex's hand tightened in mine. The creatures were small and walked upright, but hunched over. They had long pointy noses and beady little eyes. They wore old tunics and strange gilded armor. The tiny creatures came out of the shadows and studied us.

Eleanor spoke to them in French. "These are my friends," she said. "They are the Molemen. They've been here as long as me, even longer. They play wonderful games and music."

One of the Molemen spoke to her and she nodded. "They want to know if you will be working with your Aunt Perrine – The Lady Perrine?" Eleanor asked.

I had no idea what they were talking about so I answered as best I could. "We'll help her as much as we can," I said.

A loud cheer rang out in the hall and then suddenly it filled with Molemen and Molewomen carrying instruments, tables, and food.

"They like you and they salute you as the heirs of Chateau Larcher. The next Lords of the castle," Eleanor said.

Music filled the hall and mole people shoved large

goblets of a sticky sweet nectar into our hands. The mole people danced around our feet and occasionally stopped to say something to us in French. I smiled at them and pretended to understand.

"They have been the defenders of this place since long before my time," Eleanor said. "They've been here since the ancients built the first dolmen in honor of the spirits that keep it."

"What's a dolmen?" I asked.

"You haven't seen the dolmen?"

Alex and I both shook our heads.

"You have much to learn before you take the chateau," she said.

One of the Molemen pulled at my shirt and I kneeled down so I could hear him better. He handed me a necklace of some sort. It was a cross with a dragon on it. It was beautiful, like the gilded breastplates the Molemen wore. It looked like one of the amulets from the magic game I used to play back home. I gave the amulet back to the Moleman, but he only seemed frustrated by me. The music continued and the Moleman spoke to me urgently, as if he was saying something very important.

I looked up at Eleanor desperately, hoping she might translate, but she was dancing with the Molewomen. Her skirts were up and she was laughing merrily. The Moleman kept talking and occasionally his voice rose to a yell and then he put the amulet back in my hand and bowed to me.

Alex watched the entire exchange with curiosity. "Wow," he said. "Is this really happening?"

"It has to be," I answered. "Doesn't it?"

I gazed at the beautiful gold cross amulet in my hand. The dragon in the center of it was holding an enormous ruby. I held it for a few moments and then reluctantly placed it around my neck.

The music continued and a Molewoman danced around Alex. He laughed. I hadn't seen him laugh since our parents died. He smiled as two Molewomen pulled him away from me and he began to dance. The music was sweet and energetic. The Molemen played flutes and strange stringed instruments that wove together a music so sweet, I could have forgotten all my worries. The church bell above us rang, once, twice, three times, and the music stopped. The Molemen looked upwards and removed their hats. They muttered something and bowed to us as they vanished into their black tunnels. It all ended as quickly as it began. By the time the bells had rung seven times the hall was as quiet as it had been to start.

"It's time to return to pray," Eleanor explained. "They always pray when the bell strikes seven. We should go."

Eleanor led us back through the darkness and into the light where she became little more than a whisper again. "Did you like my friends?"

"Very much," I answered.

"Will you come see me again?"

"We would love too," Alex said.

"There is so much more to show you and it's been so long since I've had other children to play with," she said in a soft, almost sad voice.

I could hear Aunt Perrine's voice calling to us somewhere in the distance. "We should go," I said.

"Come see me tomorrow," Eleanor said. A strong wind blew and she vanished, leaving us wondering if she had ever been there at all. Alex and I both looked at each other and then walked, in complete silence, back home.

I think we both wondered if we had imagined it all. It seemed completely impossible. Ghosts? Molemen? The only thing that kept me from completely dismissing our afternoon as a vivid daydream was the amulet I had put around my neck. Its weight reminded me that it might have been real.

Alex and I stepped in to the warm smell of food. Our portion of the castle, our new home, was bright and cheery. The windows were still open and Aunt Perrine had moved the table out to the lawn in front of the house.

"Bonjour!" Aunt Perrine exclaimed as we entered. "I have dinner."

"Bonjour," I answered pleasantly. The food smelled wonderful.

"Wash your 'ands and I we will eat outside."

Alex and I washed in silence and sat down at the pretty lawn outside the castle. Our plates were piled high with some kind of beans and sausage. There was bread and some sort of vegetable mix to go with it.

"Eat, eat," Aunt Perrine said. "You boys look like you 'ave been 'aving an adventure."

"Oh, we have!" Alex exclaimed.

"Oh la la. You will have to tell me all about it."

I sat down and tasted the food. It was delicious. I smiled and filled my mouth with more food as Alex explained our day to Aunt Perrine. Aunt Perrine nodded and smiled as she ate and listened. She had a full glass of red wine and she drank deeply and seemed to be taking Alex's story very seriously.

Alex smiled as he talked. He was thrilled and I ate happily, because for the first time since Mom and Dad died, Alex and I were having fun. When he had finished telling the story, Alex ate enthusiastically and Aunt Perrine was silent.

Finally," she said. "I'm glad to see you boys settling in and I'm glad you are both 'appy 'ere."

"This is good," Alex said as he ate. "I think Mom used to make this sometimes. What is it?" Chunks of food fell out of his mouth as he attempted to eat and talk at the same time. His speech was garbled and the food stuck to his shirt. I shriveled my nose in disgust and looked away.

I took another bite and realized Mom did used to make it. I couldn't believe I had forgotten. How could I forget? It was Dad's favorite.

Aunt Perrine smiled as she talked. She always seemed so happy. "It's Cassolette. Is very good. Your father always loved my Cassolette."

The sun set over the castle gates painting the courtyard a bright pink and then faded. We helped Aunt Perrine clean and she sang as she cleaned.

Night came and Aunt Perrine watched us go upstairs to get ready for bed. When we were done, she told us a story.

"*Once upon a time...*" she said. "All stories start with once upon a time...*There was a queen who had been born poor. Fate had made her quick witted and she had married far above her station, but her husband was dim witted and was a very poor ruler. The king and queen had a baby, a beautiful baby girl whom they both loved. There were many who envied the happiness of the king and queen and their lovely baby. One of these was the mighty green dragon Verdi. Verdi was clever and hated the king's stupidity. He thought it a cruel twist of fate that such land and wealth and such a brilliant queen should be given to a dimwit. So this clever dragon devised a plan to expose the king and set the queen on the throne...*"

"But why did the dragon care?" Alex asked.

"He didn't really. Dragons never do, but dragons sometimes will destroy things that offer them even the mildest irritation. Most dragons hate people and are easily provoked. *Time passed and the dragon made his plans. He planned to trick the king. The dragon told the king that if he brought his daughter to him, he would show him how to find a mountain of gold. The king was also greedy, so he quickly agreed.*

31

"When the queen found out that her daughter was missing, she searched everywhere for her little girl. When she realized there was no help to be had in finding the little girl, she went to the tower and fetched a book of old spells. She cast the old magic, and using that magic, she found the dragon. But it was too late. The young girl had already been devoured and the king entombed in his mountain of gold, but the queen was angry so she spun a spell so powerful that the ground itself shook. The stones of heaven fell down onto earth and when the dragon realized what he had done, he shuddered, for the queen's spell killed not just him, but all dragons everywhere. The very earth opened up and swallowed them whole. It devoured them as the dragon had devoured the queen's daughter.

"But fate is not without a sense of humor and the queen's daughter was cursed to walk the earth until the queen herself died. The princess would never know rest, until the sorceress queen died. The princess was cursed to be a ghost until the sorceress gave up her magic immortality."

"So why didn't the queen just give up her immortality?" I asked.

"Zat is a story for anozer night," Aunt Perrine said.

Alex grimaced. "That's a terrible story."

"Not all stories 'ave 'appy endings."

"Well I don't like it," Alex said.

"I vill tell you one with a 'appy ending tomorrow," Aunt Perrine promised, and she kissed Alex's head.

I looked out the window and thought about Eleanor and wondered if she had been a princess. I wondered if all the fairytales were true. If dragons hadn't once tricked silly kings and if princesses hadn't once been lost to the dragons' terrible jaws.

Chapter 4

Skeletons in the Attic

The banging started in the middle of the night again. I woke up and found Alex sitting apprehensively on the edge of my bed. He was looking at me with wide, horrified eyes.

"If Eleanor is a ghost and she's real," he whispered, "then why can't there really be something horrible in the attic?"

There were tears in his eyes and I scooted over and made room for him in bed with me.

"You can stay here, but you have to go to sleep," I demanded. Alex crawled in next to me and closed his eyes.

But we couldn't sleep. The banging upstairs turned into rattling and then into yelling. Alex and I could only lay on the bed watching the ceiling and wondering what hideous creature was going to come stumbling down the stairs to eat us.

"I wish Dad was here," Alex said.

"Me too."

There was another thud and then more commotion. This time they were speaking in English. I could almost hear them. I heard someone shout, "Bed," and then someone say something that sounded like, "Be quiet."

Bang. Bang. Bang. Someone stomped down the stairs and then someone even bigger followed them. Alex scooted closer to me in the bed. I could feel his tension. I put my hand in his. I could almost hear his heart pounding over the sound of his ragged breath.

Thud. They were right outside the door. Crack. They were breaking things. I sat up.

"I forgot to lock the door!" Alex whimpered.

I looked at the doorknob in terror. I was too afraid to get up. Alex looked at me with pleading eyes so I summoned all the courage in my body and rose to my feet.

Thud. Something banged right into the door, making the door shake. There were voices. I could hear what they were saying.

"I told you not to touch my stuff," someone said.

"I didn't touch anything," the other voice complained.

"Yeah. Well then who moved my book?"

"I wouldn't touch your ridiculous book."

There was another bang and then a muffled yell and I pushed my ear against the door straining to hear what they were saying.

"They sound like kids," I said. "They sound like us."

"What?" Alex asked.

"They don't sound like monsters. They're fighting like we do."

"So? Monsters can fight."

"Yeah. But not like this. What if they're kid ghosts, like Eleanor?"

"Eleanor wouldn't make that much racket."

"I'm gonna look outside."

"Don't you dare! Just lock the door!"

"I don't think they're monsters."

"No!"

I opened the door and looked out into the dimly lit hallway. I couldn't see much, the chair, some old paintings. Bang. Two figures fell onto the floor fighting. One of them was nothing but bones and a grimacing skull and the other had sharp teeth and gleaming red eyes.

"Ahhhhh!" I screamed

"Ahhhhh!" Alex screamed.

"Ahhhhh!" The monsters screamed.

The red-eyed beast stood up and tried to run backwards, falling down the stairs. The skeleton stood up, but his head fell off. He grabbed it awkwardly and ran towards us with his skull in his hands.

I think Alex panicked, because when he started to run he ran towards the skeleton instead of away from it and the two collided in the middle of the hall. Alex began to dash down the stairs, but the skeleton's skull became caught on the drawstring of Alex's pants so the two ran together screaming down the rest of the stairs, leaving the skeleton's body bumping into things in the hall.

I stopped screaming and chased after my brother, who was jumping up and down and screaming in the kitchen.

"Get it off me! Get it off me! Get it off me!" he yelled as he jumped up and down.

"Ahhhhh!" the skeleton continued to scream.

I yanked the skull off Alex's pants, screaming when the skeleton looked at me with its black eyes.

"Put it in the oven!" Alex yelled. He opened the door and I threw the skull in the oven.

I wiped my hands on my pants and hopped around. "What was that?"

Alex turned all the knobs on the oven. "I don't know!"

We both stared at the oven wide eyed and stunned, just when we thought we had won, the red-eyed creature ran in the room. The monster was tall and thin with a white face and long shinning teeth. It pushed Alex aside and opened the oven, retrieving the skeleton head. The skull was screaming and it must have been hot because the other monster juggled it like a hot potato before he dropped it on the floor.

"What did you do that for?" demanded the monster. He stared at us.

Stunned, I answered him. "He was a skeleton."

The monster picked up the skull with a dishtowel decorated with pictures of kittens, which had been hanging by the sink. He held the skull like a baby and patted it. The skeleton only scowled at him.

"I'm not a baby. Stop that and put me back on my body!" the skeleton shouted.

"Don't shout at me! This is your fault!"

"How is it my fault? You pushed me down the stairs!"

"Well you woke the kids up with all your yelling," the monster answered.

"You are always messing with my stuff," the skeleton retorted.

"If you feel that way, I'll just put you right back in the oven."

The monster opened the oven door and the skeleton, or skull, or head, wailed in dismay. "Fine. It's my fault. Just put me back on my body."

"Not until you say you are sorry."

"I'm sorry."

"What's wrong with you two?" I bellowed.

Both monsters stopped their fighting and looked at Alex and me. Alex kicked me in the back of the leg and I flinched.

"What did you do that for?" he hissed.

"They're driving me crazy," I hissed back.

The toilet in the other room flushed and all four of us turned to look at the door into the living room. A light came on, a door slammed and the two monsters looked mortified.

"Listen," the monster explained. "Don't tell on us, OK?"

"Tell on you?" I asked in disbelief.

"Don't tell Lady Perrine how much noise we were making. In fact, please don't tell her we're here," the skull pleaded.

The monster looked around and slid under the table clutching the skull to his chest like a football. The kitchen light flickered on and Aunt Perrine came into the kitchen in her hot pink, knitted robe. She looked like she was still half asleep and she yawned conspicuously as she entered the kitchen.

"What're you two doing up?" She asked. "It's 4 am."

For a moment, both Alex and I looked around like idiots

and then Alex opened his mouth and found something to say. "I was thirsty."

"Why is ze oven open?" Aunt Perrin asked.

"We were hungry too," I said.

I could see the monsters under the table and all I could think was that if those two were that bad at hiding, why did it take us two days to find them? The monsters' feet were sticking out and if Aunt Perrine even looked down it would be obvious they were there. But Aunt Perrine didn't look down. She shuffled over to the oven and closed the door. "If you are 'ungry, you should 'ave a cookie. Don't cook. It iz dangerous to in ze middle of ze night."

She shuffled away leaving Alex and I staring stupidly at the monsters under the table. The monster stood up and smiled at me. I wasn't sure what to think. It looked more like a grimace than a smile and he had about a hundred razor sharp teeth.

"Thanks," he said.

"Anytime," I answered.

"I'm Uno and this is Roger, but I call him Jolly Roger." He laughed.

"Shut up," the skull complained. "My name is just Roger."

"Just Jolly Roger," the monster taunted.

"You two live here?" I asked.

"Yeah. We live here," the skull answered. "Not always, but we have for a while."

"Where'd you live before?" Alex queried.

"Here and there," the skull replied. "I used to live in America. Some stupid teenagers dug me up and tried to cast some lame spell to bring me back to life and here I am. Alive...kind of. They ran away and left me."

"That stinks," I said.

"Yeah."

"I'm a vampire," Uno said. "I'm from New York. I used to have a family, parents, a house, and then some jerk bit me and now I glow in the dark."

"What a jerk," I said.

There was an uncomfortable silence as we all stared at each other. I really had no idea what to think or say.

"So, you just live up in the attic and fight all night now and drink diet blood?" Alex asked.

"Sometimes we go out," Uno explained.

"We do stuff," Roger added. "Sometimes we help Lady Perrine. Sometimes we go see the other folk around here."

Alex scratched his head. "Like who? Eleanor?"

The skull scrunched up his face in something that looked like anger, although I had trouble telling because of his bony features. "Yeah."

"How'd you get here?"

"Lady Perrine saved us," Roger said.

I studied Roger. "From who?"

"The slayers. You know, those guys that go around trying to kill monsters, ghosts, and magic folk."

I raised my eyebrows. "People do that?"

Roger nodded emphatically. "Yeah, but it's safe here."

There was another silence and then Uno smiled and moved towards the stairs. "Well," he said. "Nice meeting you. I should probably go put Roger together again. Goodnight."

Uno tripped a little as he walked and as soon as they vanished up the stairs, they started fighting again. For a while, Alex just watched the space where the two monsters had been and then we looked at each other and started laughing.

I laughed. "I can't believe we were afraid of that!"

We laughed all the way upstairs. I fell asleep with a grin on my face and for the first time in a very long time, I honestly couldn't wait for morning.

Alex was up long before me. I could hear him upstairs in the loft talking to Roger. It was hot and I had sweated through my pajamas in the night. There was no air conditioning and summer had been mild, but the weather changed. I peeled off my pajamas and threw on a t-shirt and shorts.

It was early and I stumbled up into the loft. Alex and Roger were lying on the floor playing a game of Checkers. Uno was resting on the bed reading a book. It was a strange scene – a skeleton and a little boy playing checkers. It could have been a picture from summer camp, if it hadn't have been for the horrible monsters.

"What're you doing?" I asked.

"Roger's gonna show me where we can going swimming today," Alex said.

"OK. Do you swim a lot Roger?" I was half astonished and half just being polite.

"Not in a while. Mr. Vampire there doesn't do well in the sun and I don't like going alone."

I looked at Alex. "I thought we were going to see Eleanor today?"

Uno looked surprised. "You met Eleanor?"

"Yeah," I answered.

Roger rolled on his back and laughed.

"What's so funny?" Uno demanded.

"Uno has a crush on Eleanor, but she won't give him the time of *day*. Get it. Time of *day*." Roger laughed again.

Uno frowned. "I do not,"

"How old are you guys?" I asked.

"I don't know," Roger replied. "It's hard for me to keep count. I was ten when I died. I don't keep count anymore."

"Oh," I said. "I'm sorry."

Roger shrugged. "You get used to it after a while. Aunt

Perrine makes us cake to celebrate the first day we came here."

I thought for a minute. "Can you eat?"

Roger was quick to answer. "Kind of."

"It's disgusting," Uno said. "It falls out of his ribs, but he just keeps on eating."

"At least I can eat. Uno gets blood cake for his special days. It looks like raw meat."

"It is pretty vile," Uno admitted with a shrug. "I love it though."

"So what are we doing today?" Alex interrupted.

"We haven't decided," I said. "We were going to go swimming or perhaps to see Eleanor."

"Why can't we do both?" Alex asked. "I mean, I had a question for Eleanor too."

"Let's see Eleanor first," I suggested.

"I'm going too," Uno said.

"You'll burn up," Roger said.

"I'll wear my cloak."

"You'll look stupid, Uno."

"You look stupid all the time."

"Just shut up and get ready," I said. "I'm going to eat breakfast. I'll meet you all by the keep in an hour."

With that, I ran down stairs to find Aunt Perrine. Aunt Perrine was in the kitchen, as always, drinking coffee and humming to herself. She had shed her usual sweaters and was wearing a t-shirt with pink flowers and kittens on it. She wore her hair down and it spilled over her shoulders in long, gray curls.

"Bonjour!" she said cheerfully. "You had a long night, no?"

"Yes," I said.

She put a bowl of cereal in front of me and I sat down to eat it. As I ate, she sat down and watched me. She looked at me intensely as if she was trying to read my face and I looked at her with the same intensity.

I realized that she must have been pretty in her youth. She had clear, blue eyes and fine features. She was fat and squat, but with the fat gone, she would have been lovely. Her crinkled hands were covered with pretty rings that looked as old as the castle. With her knitted hat removed, I could see that she had long, curly hair. It was nice.

I knew what I wanted to ask her, but the words were stuck in my throat. The questions seemed silly – childish – but I had to know.

"Is this castle magic?" I asked.

"Bien sur," she said. "It is magic."

"Are you magic?"

"What do you zink, little prince?"

"You have to be."

Aunt Perrine only grinned.

"What are you?" I asked stupidly.

"All in good time, little prince. All in good time. Now is ze time for you and your brozer to learn French. You cannot go to school without French. Come."

I followed her into the living room. There was an old table with clawed feet in the corner and the top of it had been covered with workbooks and a CD player. She pointed and I sat down. She opened the workbook. The book was called *Beginning with French*. Aunt Perrine hit play. The voice on the other end of the CD said, "Bonjour." I answered it.

"Alex," Aunt Perrine called. "Alex!" She vanished out of the room; I was left listening to the CD and writing simple French phrases in my workbook. After a few minutes, Aunt Perrine returned dragging Alex behind her. He had a scowl on his face and seemed deeply unhappy. Aunt Perrine pressed a button and the CD began again. "Bonjour," the voice said. I answered it, but Alex scowled and sank deeper in his chair.

"I have to go out now," Aunt Perrine said. "If you do your work, I will 'ave a special treat for you when I return. Work 'ard."

She waved and I heard the front door close behind her. As soon as the door shut, Alex turned the CD player off.

"Let's go," he said.

"But our lessons...we need to learn French."

"You're such a killjoy."

"Aunt Perrine is our guardian now and we have to respect her. We can't go off and do whatever we want. She told us to study."

"Blah, blah, blah," Alex said. "That's all I hear you saying and I'm going to see Eleanor with or without you. Have fun with the French."

It only took me a few seconds to decide to follow him. I wanted to study, but there was no way I was going to let my little brother explore all the magic in the castle while I was stuck inside saying bonjour to a CD player.

Chapter 5

The Old Ones

It didn't take me long to catch up with Alex. He was running across the courtyard to the keep. Uno was already there, wearing a ridiculous looking cape that covered his entire body, only leaving a small slit for his eyes. He looked like a cartoon picture of death from an old comic book. He could have been scary, if he hadn't of tripped on his own robes on the way up the spiral stairs. It was like watching a toddler in clothes that were too big. He fell at least four times.

Roger caught up with us on the way up. He got there just in time to watch Uno fall flat on his face.

"Good one!" Roger yelled.

Somehow, we made it to the top of the stairs and went into Eleanor's room. The sun was shining brightly in the window. I pulled the curtains closed so we could see her. She came from nowhere and materialized out of dust and shadow. There was a small smile on her lips. "Good morning," she said softly. She curtsied.

I bowed to her out of instinct. "I trust you are well this morning."

"Very well," I answered honestly. "And you?"

"I'm better now that you are here to keep me company." She looked around and saw Roger and Uno in the corner and her face twisted in snobbish contempt. "What're you two doing here?"

"Sorry, Your Highness," Roger said. "Didn't mean to soil your filthy room with our feet."

"What's wrong with them?" Alex asked defensively.

"They know why I'm mad," Eleanor said.

44

"Say you're sorry, Roger."

"No," Roger said.

Eleanor colored up. "If you can't apologize you can leave."

Roger's bony lips twisted into something that resembled a frown. "This isn't your castle."

"But it's my room and I want you to leave," Eleanor insisted.

Roger threw up his hands. "Fine. I'm sorry. I'm sorry. I'm sorry. Are you happy?"

Eleanor smiled. "Yes."

An uncomfortable silence filled the room. Eleanor kept smiling like a Cheshire cat, and Roger scowled and pouted like Alex when he didn't get his way. I really wasn't sure what was going on or why Roger was sorry. I was completely confused. "Why is he sorry, Uno?"

"Last time we saw Eleanor she said she was a princess. He told her she was a liar. He said everything she said was a lie."

"Was she really lying?" I asked.

"Who knows?" Uno answered. "She's been here forever. She could make up any stories she wanted, couldn't she? It doesn't matter. I like her either way."

"You are common, Roger, and I'm your better and you should treat me with respect," Eleanor said.

"I am no more common than you," Roger argued.

"Yes, you are."

"It doesn't matter," Alex said. "We're common too. No one is royalty any more. Who cares anyway?"

"No, Alex, You are wrong. You are everything but common. You are the heirs of this kingdom. You are lords," Eleanor said passionately.

I laughed despite the seriousness of Eleanor's tone. I couldn't help myself. Lords of what? Lords of a rubble?

Orphan kings of a broken castle in a village in the middle of nowhere? And we were hardly lords of even the rubble.

"I can go if you just came to laugh at me." As soon as the words were said, Eleanor began to fade away. She vanished as if she had never been there at all and only the memory of her remained. I had almost forgotten that she was a ghost until she faded away. I peered into the darkness looking for any piece of her in the shadows.

"Wait!" Alex cried. "Don't go! My brother's an idiot. He didn't mean to hurt your feelings."

"I'm sorry for laughing," I muttered. "I really didn't mean to be rude. I just don't see myself as a lord."

She looked at our faces and smiled. "All right, but those two can't come with us."

Eleanor became bright again – a light in the darkness. She glided across the room to stand as close to Alex and me, and as far from Roger and Uno, as she could. She scowled at them and crossed her arms.

"They are our friends," Alex protested. "Roger said he was sorry. Can't you just pretend they're our servants or something?"

"Oh," Eleanor said softly. "I guess that's fine."

"I am no one's serving person," Roger declared and with that, he made an ugly face at Eleanor and ran down the stairs.

Uno stayed on inching slowly closer to Eleanor.

Eleanor watched Roger go with a hint of anger.

We could all hear Roger as he stumbled down the stairs and out of the door. The door slammed shut, with a bang and I could almost hear him as he stomped through the courtyard and back into our little portion of the castle. I felt bad for him. I imagined him going up to his attic and sitting alone surrounded by cans of diet blood and old board games. It seemed like a pretty depressing way to spend your day.

"You shouldn't treat him like that," I said.

Eleanor cast me a wicked glance. "Why not?"

"Because he's a good guy and because we're alone in this castle. We should be nice to each other."

Eleanor's face softened a little. I almost thought she was going to call after him. "I'll be nicer to him next time."

"Thank you," I said.

Eleanor smiled. "Would you like me to show you more of my friends?"

I nodded eagerly, but Alex had something else on his mind.

"I was wondering…" he spoke hesitantly. It was a tone that wasn't common for Alex. "I, um…" His voice trailed off and we waited. "…You're dead. And I just wanted to know if you ever see any other dead people while you are, you know, being a ghost in the ghost world?"

Eleanor's eyes filled with genuine empathy. "I'm just a ghost," she whispered. "A phantom. I have no more power or knowledge than you."

"But you must know something," Alex said. "You died. What happened after you died?"

"I think I was supposed to leave. I should have followed the light, but my mother was weeping, so I stayed and the light faded and I stayed here."

"So, don't other people stay here? Can't we find the other people that didn't follow the light?"

"Alex," I said. "Mom and Dad are dead…"

"So is Uno. So is Roger. So is Eleanor, but they are all still here. Why can't Mom and Dad be?"

"You have to let them go," I said gently. "They are in a better place."

"Don't say that! Why do people always say that! You don't know that. You've never been dead, but Eleanor has."

"I don't know how to find other ghosts," Eleanor said.

"There has to be a way." Alex's eyes filled with tears.

Eleanor frowned. "Maybe there is."

"How?"

"The old ones know the old magic. They know many things of this world and the next. Maybe they can tell us."

I didn't like the way she said, "the old ones." They sounded like the type of creatures you wouldn't want to visit. They didn't even have real names and I couldn't trust anything that didn't have a name. The old ones sounded dangerous.

"Where do we find them?" Alex asked.

"They aren't far. They live by the dolmen and the ancient places of old magic."

"Isn't this place ancient."

"It's old," Eleanor said. "But I lived here. No, the ancient places were here before the English, the Franks or the Gauls. They were here before the Romans or the Celts. They were here in the twilight time, before men wrote. In those dark years, people worshipped the old ones and built the dolmen, to honor them. They buried their dead beneath them. They say there are many people buried there. "

The thought of old stones on top of lots of dead people didn't sound like a fun day in the sun to me and it certainly didn't sound like a good idea. In fact, it sounded like a completely crazy idea. I couldn't think of a much worse idea than marching off into the woods to look for old spirits on top of a bunch of dead people. "I don't like this, Alex."

"Where are the dolmens?" Alex asked.

"They aren't far, just past the village, in the old woods," Eleanor answered.

"Will you take us?"

Eleanor hesitated and looked down at the ground. She was unsure. "The old ones can be crabby."

Alex was more determined than I had seen him in a long time. His jaw was set the way it used to get when he told Mom he didn't want to eat broccoli. "I don't care," he said.

I shook my head. "We can't do this."

"Don't you want to even try to see them again?" Alex implored. "Don't you miss them at all?"

"I do, but...but..." I couldn't think of anything else to say.

"I'll take you," Eleanor said. "But don't tell your Aunt."

We followed Eleanor down the stairs and out of the castle. We followed her into the village where the villagers gave us strange looks. It was morning and most of the people must have been at work, because only a few people were out. Some greeted us with a hesitant *bonjour*, but others saw Uno in his robes and looked at us as if we were just a little bit loony.

It didn't take long to walk through the narrow, cobbled streets of the medieval village to its edge. The village ended but the road continued on through lush farmland covered in sunflowers and grape vines. Occasional farmhouses dotted the landscape. We walked through the farmlands to the end of the pavement. The road ended abruptly and the woods began. Tall, dark trees toured over us like giants staring down at us with angry eyes. The main road was made of gravel and it widened a little, but Eleanor took us off it and down a hidden path into the deeper parts of the woods.

There were many dolmen along the path. Small dolmen were little more than piles of rock, but at the end of the path were five large stones piled up to make a table and they were surrounded by a circle of even larger stones. The woods parted for these old stones, the grass thin and dotted with tiny flowers.

I stopped on the edge of the circle and looked in

pensively. There was an eerie silence about the place. There
were no birds, no animals, and no wind. It wasn't natural.

Eleanor walked into the circle and sat on one of the large
stones. Alex followed her and stood beside her. Uno stood
on the edge of the circle like me.

"This isn't a good idea," Uno whispered. "Bad things happen when people mess with magic they don't understand. Look at Roger. That's what happens when people mess with stuff. Poor Roger."

Eleanor stood on the stone and a cloud passed in front of the sun, making the forest dark. Everything was still and Eleanor became luminous in the dark. She raised her arms and extended them to the woods. She spoke in a language I had never heard and then she sat back down.

I looked around. Alex seemed nervous. He chewed his nails when he was nervous. Before our parents died, I always tried to avoid Alex as much as I could. He was never into the things I was into. He liked sports and spent most of his time riding his bike or playing ball. It had always irritated me that he was as big as I was even though he was younger. I had a few friends and we were pretty tight, but Alex always acted like he ran the whole neighborhood. Generally, Alex drove me nuts. I had thought he was spoiled, irritable, and annoying, and he thought I was a, know-it-all, bossy, killjoy. But looking at him in the field chewing his nails, I felt sorry for him. So I stepped into the circle with him.

A wind passed through the leaves of the trees and the clouds thickened. I could hear branches crunching and cracking in the distance and leaves rustling on the ground. There was a whisper of wings, like birds flying away.

Eleanor smiled. "They are coming," she said.

"What are they?" I asked.

"Wait," she said.

At first, I didn't see them. The trees moved. I saw them move, but I thought it was a trick of the light. Alex stepped back and I could see the fear in his eyes. The forest swayed and the trees grew limbs. I suppressed a yell that got caught in my throat. I didn't want Eleanor to know how afraid I was. Alex gasped. The trees turned into living beings. The beings had faces like people, but bodies like trees. They were part of the forest. Their long limbs moved and swayed and propelled them forward. Eyes stared out of the bark and into the shadowy wood that surrounded us. The old ones were everywhere. They were the bushes and the shrubs and the trees and they surrounded us. The leader was a woman or, at least, she was shaped like a woman. She had long leafy hair and birds nested in her tresses. Her eyes were green as the grass and her lips were pretty and red.

"Eleanor," the woman said. "Here again? Have we not warned you?"

"I did not come for myself, My Lady."

The woman looked at Alex and me and raised a single, mossy eyebrow. "Time has passed so quickly," she said. "A thousand years has come and gone and now it's time to start again."

"My Lady?"

"Tell your mother that Angerboda walks again," the woman said. "I see Perrine has already chosen her heirs."

Eleanor looked bewildered by what they were saying. "I don't understand."

"It is not yours to reason why, little phantom. We speak and you do. Thus it has always been. You must tell your mother Angerboda walks again."

"Yes, My Lady," Eleanor answered.

"Alex..." The woman turned to my brother. "You have come with questions." Her voice was like the wind, like birds flying away. Bugs crawled along her arms. Ladybugs climbed up her legs. Flowers grew at her feet.

"Y-yes," Alex stammered.

"What have you to ask Druantia the Forgotten?"

"I...I," he stammered again and stepped backwards.

"I...I want to know...if there are other...ghosts?"

"You seek your parents?" she said.

"Yes."

"I am of this earth and this life. I do not know the dead."

Druantia turned to leave, but Alex chased after her. "Please, don't you know anything that could help me?"

"The dead bring danger with them. Not all ghosts are sweet like Eleanor. Not all skeletons are funny like Roger. Be careful what you seek."

Alex was desperate. "Please."

"Light the Lantern of the Dead. It will guide lost spirits home."

Alex nodded and stepped backwards again. Druantia turned to leave, but before she vanished she leaned towards me and her body grew long so that even though her feet were rooted to the ground she could whisper in my ear. "Be brave, little prince," she said. "It is a dark road before you."

With that Druantia and her army of old ones moved back to the forest. They raised their arms and grew back into the ground until they became the very trees that protected the dolmen.

The air grew cold and the wind blew. I shivered. The clouds parted and the sun shone down on us like nothing at all had happened.

"Wow," I said.

Eleanor began to drift away from the stone circle. Her light flickered in the shade of the trees. "I like Druantia. I used to come here all the time, but she says she is too old and too forgotten for this world. She says I should let her rest."

I reached out and touched the tree that had once been Druantia. "But you don't let her rest?"

Eleanor hopped down off the rock. She was barely

visible in the noonday light. "Sometimes I do get lonely," she confessed. "It has been so many years. She remembers the old days, when my father was lord of the land and I was betrothed to one of the king's sons. I was going to be important, a princess. She remembers the good days, before the dragons and the fire."

"Dragons?" I asked, remembering Aunt Perrine's story.

"Before all the wars and battles," Eleanor continued. "She remembers how it was."

"I guess it must be lonely up there in that tower. Can't you cross over now...now that your mother is gone?" I asked.

Eleanor laughed and shrugged. "We should go back. Your Aunt will be back soon. She might notice you are gone."

There were so many questions I wanted to ask Eleanor. So many things I had to know. Why did everyone keep calling me little prince? Why did the Molemen give me the cross. Why did Druantia tell her to tell her mother about Angerboda? Who was Angerboda? But before I could open my mouth to speak, Alex was standing beside Eleanor.

"Where's the lantern of the dead?" he asked her.

"Not far from the castle. In the village. In the cemetery. You have to light it at night."

I cast a harsh glance at Alex. "At night? Oh no, don't even say it, Alex, because there is no way we are going to the cemetery at night to try to call back the dead. We are not doing it. End of story."

I began walking back to the castle and everyone followed me. I was walking as fast as I could without running. Alex caught up to me and walked with me. He looked at me with his biggest puppy eyes, but he knew enough not to say anything.

"When I was young," Eleanor said. "They used to light

the Lantern of the Dead for funerals, and on All Soul's Day, but never at night. That's why it had no power. We had power. My mother and I knew the secret magic, but we had to be quiet or we would be called witches. Eleanor of Aquitaine's mother came here once and was so impressed by mother and me that she named her after me..."

I stopped dead in my tracks and looked at the fading ghost. She looked like a child in the sunlight. She looked even younger than Alex.

"But you said that you were named after Eleanor of Aquitaine?" I said angrily.

"I did? Sometimes I forget things. I meant that she was named after me."

"When did you live in the castle?"

Eleanor looked up in the air above her as if she was searching for an answer. "1012."

"I read a book about France on the plane and it said the Eleanor of Aquitaine lived in the 1200s or something like that. You were dead a long time before her."

Eleanor opened her mouth and then closed it. She shrugged her shoulders. "I lie sometimes," she said. "It was all so long ago and hardly anyone ever listens to me in any case. I didn't think it mattered."

"I am so sick of all this," I said. I stomped away down the road to the castle leaving everyone else behind.

I trudged all the way back to the castle, thinking about how irritating all of the monsters and ghosts and spirits were. I thought that it would be better if I learned French and found some nice, normal friends down in the village.

I walked in the house, sat down at the table and turned on the CD. "Bonjour," it said. And I answered back because sometimes it is better to sit alone talking to a CD player.

Chapter 6

The Lantern of the Dead

I didn't know where Alex went. I didn't even care. I spent the next hour practicing my French. I learned how to say *How are you?* and *Where is the bathroom?* I learned how to say a lot, when Aunt Perrine came in, I was happy to show her everything I had learned.

She sat with me and listened and checked my work. "Very good," she said and slapped her hands together in delight.

"It is too bad your brozer didn't study," Aunt Perrine said with a sigh. She opened a bag and gave me my special treat. It was incredible and it wasn't little. It was a small replica of an old castle with tiny knights, ogres and monsters. Each piece was perfect in its detail and the castle was so realistic I could almost see the moss on the gray stone.

"You like?" Aunt Perrine asked.

"I love it." I threw my arms around her and hugged her. She hugged me back.

"I'm very glad you and your brozer are 'ere," she said sweetly.

"Me too. I mean, out of every place we could have ended up, this is the best."

"Merci."

She took me in the kitchen and we ate a lunch of fresh bread, strange cheese, ham, and fruit. It was delicious. Even the Orangina was pretty good. I told Aunt Perrine about our life as we ate. I told her about our little house just outside the city and about our school. I told her about my friends and karate. I even told her about my favorite video games. She listened attentively.

"Do you miss it terribly?" she asked.

"Yeah," I said. "I do. Sometimes I miss it so bad my chest hurts, but it's not so bad here and you are really nice."

"Merci. And what about brozer?"

"He misses our parents. He was always a little impulsive, but he's gone a little bonkers lately."

"Bonkers?"

"Yeah. You know, crazy?"

"Oh, yes. We all go crazy sometimes."

I looked at Aunt Perrine and wondered how many secrets she kept hidden in the old castle. I knew nothing about Chateau Larcher. I didn't even know when it was built. Big Foot could be hiding The Holy Grail in the basement for all I knew. "Tell me something about this castle. How old is it?"

"Zey built zee first walls around 900 and zey didn't finish until 1066."

"It's a strange place."

"Every place 'as secrets if you 'ave zee eyes too look."

"My mom used to say that."

"Your mamman was a very smart woman."

Aunt Perrine seemed to like my mom. She smiled when she talked about her. She spoke with such fondness it seemed like they would have wanted to spend more time together. You would think they would have looked for every chance to visit and talk. I thought Aunt Perrine was someone my mother would have loved. I couldn't imagine what fight my father could have had with her to keep them apart for so long. "What did you and my father fight over?" I asked.

"Hmmm," she said thoughtfully. "Zat's a hard question. I 'ave no children. No family. Your grandfather and I were very close. He loved me deeply and I helped your grand-mother and he care for all their children. I always felt closest to your fazer. I vanted him to have zis castle and its responsibilities. Your fazer said yes, but later changed his mind. I told him he couldn't change his mind. We fought. Zat's all. He didn't want the responsibility."

"Why not?"

"Zis castle is a lot of responsibility," she said.

"I would never turn away a gift like that," I said firmly.

She smiled. "I hope you won't."

The door slammed and Alex strolled into the room. He looked happy, but he was covered in a fine film of filth. He left a trail of mud and leaves behind him. He looked like the swamp monster.

"Oh Mon Dieu!" Aunt Perrine yelled. "To zee shower with you. Vite! Vite!"

Aunt Perrine dragged Alex upstairs and I was left alone to my thoughts. I went over the couch and sat down, it was covered in a thick fabric; on it were tiny pictures of people wearing old clothes. The pictures repeated over and over again, to form a pattern. My mother had something like it on her bedspread at home. I remembered her calling it toile. Seeing the pattern made me homesick.

Looking further about the room, there was a TV, but it was small and somehow, I just wasn't interest in TV anymore. There were a few books on the shelf. The windows stood open and the lace curtain fluttered in the soft evening breeze. It was peaceful sitting there.

Dinner came and went with a duck roasted in fat and potatoes smothered in cheese. The evening came and the sun faded, Aunt Perrine put us to bed.

"I will tell you anozer story tonight," she said as we lay on Alex's bed. "Tonight I tell

You *La Grenouillebienfaisante*. In English, it is zee kind frog. ...*Once upon a time, zere was a very good king. Zis king married a queen he loved greatly. When zee king was attacked by his enemies , he sent zee queen to safety. She was sent far away from him and was away from him for a very long time. She missed her love terribly and resolved to return, despite the guards the king had sent to make her stay away from his battles. The queen was determined. She was also clever. She had a carriage made for herself, and took advantage of a distraction to escape. In her rush, she lost control of her horses and they bolted. She was thrown from her horses and was badly injured. She lost consciousness*

"*A gigantic woman, wearing a lion skin, was zere when she woke. The giantess said she was the Fairy Lioness, and took zee queen to her home, a frightful cave crammed with ravens and owls. It had a lake filled with the most fearsome monsters. The water of the lake burned with a blue flame. There was almost no food and the queen was always hungry. Zis Lion Fairy kept zee good queen, and zee good queen drowned in her sorrows.*

"*Zee queen worked hard for the Lion Fairy, but one day she saw a raven devouring a frog. She saved the frog and the frog was so overjoyed to be alive, zat he told the queen that he would grant her any wish.*

"*The queen wept, for the Lion Fairy was cruel and harsh and the queen was pregnant. She knew when her baby was born the Lion Fairy would eat it. So she begged the frog to tell her husband where she was and how to save her.*

"*The frog was honored to help such a beautiful and kind queen, and he went many miles through many dark forests to bring the king. Zee king came with all his best knights, but he found it impossible to pass the lake of monsters. Zee king fought and fought and many nights passed, but the monsters were too strong.*

"*But the frog was wise and he knew an old dragon that lived not so far away. He went to fetch the dragon, and zee dragon promised zee king that if he gave him his first-born daughter, he would defeat the monsters. The king agreed and the queen and king were reunited.*

"Their joy was short, however, and soon zee queen gave birth to a beautiful baby girl. The dragon took the girl while the kingdom slept and for sixteen years, the kingdom mourned. So long, zat it was called the kingdom noir – the kingdom black.

"But the frog did not forget the kindness of zee queen or her beauty and he wanted to save the lovely princess. He knew the old magic. He knew dragons, so he went out and found a prince of great strength and honor. The prince was a famous monster hunter who had slain the Lion Fairy and others like her. The frog told the prince that if he killed zee dragon and cut it open he would find zee most beautiful princess in the world. The prince did as the frog said and he killed the dragon and saved the princess. The kingdom rejoiced and as a wedding present, the king gave the prince his castle, The Chateau Larcher, and the prince became king of all he saw and the frog lived with them forever in the castle. The king and queen ruled for a thousand years and were beloved of all the people."

The story ended and I looked over and saw that Alex had fallen asleep.

"Is it true?" I asked Aunt Perrine.

Aunt Perrine closed the book. "It is an old fairytale."

"But...but you said this place is magic, so couldn't it be true?"

"I zink zat all fairytales carry a piece of truth."

I yawned. It was late and I was tired. "I think it's true."

I got up, and went back to my room. I thought about Lion Fairies as I fell asleep. I dreamt of dragons and knights fighting wicked Lion Fairies and terrible monsters. I woke up and Bastet was sitting on my bed, watching me with sleepy green eyes. She purred loudly and I reached out to pet her. I knew that Alex was standing by my bed, but I tried to ignore him.

I rolled over and tried to go back to sleep, but I could hear Alex breathing. I put a pillow over my head, but he just came closer.

"Go away!" I yelled.

"I'm going to the cemetery tonight," Alex said. "And I think you should come."

I sat up in bed. "Why? Why are you doing this?"

"I never got to say goodbye," Alex said. "I just want to say goodbye."

I nodded reluctantly and getting out of bed, put on my sneakers. "Ok," I said.

The village was quiet at night. In France, everything seemed to shut down after seven. All the stores were closed. Everyone went home. There were few streetlights and darkness spread out over the village like a blanket. There were no twenty-four hour gas stations, grocery stores, or fast food restaurants. So especially in the small village of Chateau Larcher, there was a sense of utter quiet.

It wasn't cold, but I was still shivering. I'd never say it to Alex. Maybe I'd never say it at all, but I was really scared. Wandering an ancient cemetery at night looking for ghosts to me sounded like something of which most adults might be afraid. I followed my brother, because I didn't want him doing it alone. I didn't want him getting hurt.

Uno and Roger were waiting for us at the gates with candles. Uno smiled and he looked like a boy in a Halloween costume with the silly smile on his face.

"Time to call the ghosts," he said in a fake creepy voice.

Roger looked a little cross. "This stuff never works."

"It worked for you, didn't it?" Alex said.

"Well, yeah, but that was different."

"How?" I asked.

Roger smiled a strange, skeletal grin. "I don't know. I guess it isn't."

"Have you ever done anything like this before?" I asked Uno.

"Are you kidding me?" he replied. "I'm afraid of myself sometimes and I can't even see my reflection in the mirror. I think I see my reflection and jump."

I laughed and Roger made a funny face.

"So I guess we should do it?" Alex said.

No one moved to open the gate. They just stared at it. I could see the cemetery through the gate. It was pretty. There were traditional gravestones, modern stones, old angels praying over ancient graves, and graves so old they were hardly there. The Lantern of the Dead was not what I expected. When the old ones told us to light it, I had imagined it being a lamp. The lantern wasn't a lantern at all, but a large, oblong tower that reached up above the cemetery.

"I'll do it," Roger said and he pushed the gate open and walked inside. "Hello!" he called to no one in particular. "If there are any other dead people wandering around here make yourselves known!" His call was answered only by silence.

"OK then," Roger said. "It looks like Uno and I are the only living dead around. Let's go in."

Alex went in after Roger and I followed him, but Uno hesitated and looked out on the cemetery with fear.

"Are you coming?" I asked.

"I don't know."

"Why not?"

"It's a cemetery."

"Yeah," I said. "And you're a vampire. I thought vampires lived in cemeteries."

"I don't like cemeteries."

"Are you afraid?"

Uno shrugged. "A little."

"Don't you have super powers? Aren't you immortal?"

"Yeah, but we're actually much more vulnerable than you think. I mean, stakes to the heart, garlic, holy water, tanning beds, bright lights, a good blow to the head. There are a lot of things that can hurt me. I don't even think we're supposed to go on hallowed ground, technically speaking, and cemeteries are hallowed ground."

"He's a big chicken!" Roger called.

Uno didn't even argue with Roger. "I'll just watch from here."

"OK," I said and I ran to catch up with Roger.

"He's even afraid of the dark," Roger whispered in my ear.

"What? But light hurts him, doesn't it?"

"Yeah, but he's still afraid of the dark."

I walked away from Roger, who was still laughing at Uno and caught up with Alex. Alex was standing at the base of the lantern and looked up. It was beautiful in the soft light of the moon. It was covered in stone vines and angels that crept upwards to the window, where it could be lit. Alex took a deep breath.

Alex took a lighter and candle from his pocket. I didn't know where he had gotten them or even how he knew he needed them. "Lift me up."

I gave him a boost and he placed a small white candle in the stone lantern. He hesitated then lit the candle. I dropped him to the ground and he fell with a thud. We all looked out at the sky, waiting.

"Maybe you should call their names or something," Roger said.

"Mom! Dad! If you are out there, come see us!" Alex cried.

Nothing happened. I could hear Roger doing some kind of silly dance on the grass, but there was nothing else.

"Don't call them Mom and Dad. Call their real names, idiot," I said.

Alex scowled at me. "If you know so much, you do it."

"Caroline Allaire and Bastian Allaire, I call you to come and seek your sons!" I yelled.

"I knew this wouldn't work," Alex complained. He kicked the lantern and started to head out of the cemetery.

Roger followed Alex. I hesitated and looked up. There was something wrong with the sky. It was getting brighter.

"Wait!" I called. "Don't you see that?"

"No," Alex said. "This entire thing is stupid. I'm stupid."

The sky was definitely getting brighter. It wasn't just brighter. The color of the sky had changed. It was an odd shade of green. The clouds thickened and a thin mist settled over the ground. The air around us became colder. Clouds obscured the moon and the stars faded. In the dark, I could see a small light coming towards us.

"Look!" I yelled. "You don't see that?"

Everyone stopped and looked up. It was Mom and Dad. I laughed out loud. They looked like themselves, but they were luminous like Eleanor. They were made of light. I ran to Mom and tried to hug her and she smiled down on me with love. She was beautiful. I had forgotten how beautiful my mother was. Her long, black hair spilled over her shoulders framing her perfect moon-shaped face and my father looked well. He was tall and square shouldered.

"You're really here!" I yelled.

"Yes," my mother answered. "We are here, but you shouldn't be."

I had forgotten what it felt like to be scolded by my mother. It had been so long, I actually liked it. I loved being scolded. Alex ran for Mom and tried to hug her but fell in the grass instead. Mom reached out to him and somehow lifted him to his feet. She put a phantom hand on his shoulder and Alex cried with joy.

"I missed you so much," he wept.

"I know, baby, I know," Mom said.

"Why did you go?"

Mom leaned down to him and smiled at him with lips that seemed to be made from stars and then she put a hand on my shoulder. "We never wanted to leave you, my beautiful boys. We would have loved to have stayed with you forever, but God has different plans for all of us. We can't fight our destinies."

"Destiny?" Alex asked. "I don't care about destiny I just want you to stay with us."

"It is not our place to choose," my father said. He was smiling too. "We love you so much, but we can't stay."

Tears ran down Alex's face. "Why not!"

"Because you and Gabriel have a destiny. You have to be brave now, my two sons, you have to be brave."

Mom looked at me with her starry eyes. "Do you remember when I told you the world was older than time and that magic tied it all together?"

I nodded.

"I wasn't lying, was I?"

I shook my head and leaned into her.

"Now it's time for you two to find the magic in yourselves," she said.

My father joined us in our strange embrace. "Find the magic and don't ever lose hope, we are always with you, even if you can't see us. We are always with you."

"Really?" Alex asked.

"Yes," Dad said. "And you should have studied your French like Aunt Perrine told you to."

Alex looked down sheepishly. "I'll do my best."

"Now listen carefully," Mom said. "Don't do this again. This is dangerous. Do you two hear me?"

We both nodded.

Dad kissed us both on the cheek with his phantom lips. It felt like a gentle breeze. "Now we need you to run as fast as you can to the castle and close the gate."

"What?" I asked.

"You woke the dead," Mom said. "You need to run."

Their light began to fade. Alex and I looked around. The soil around the graves was moving. The dirt was shifting as if someone was trying to get out. Alex yelled and ran for the gate. I looked up at the fading image of my mom and dad.

They spoke together in unison. "We are always with you."

"Take care of your brother. You are the wiser of the two," Mom said to me and then they vanished.

The first ghoulish hand pushed its way through the soil and I began to run after Alex. Roger only smiled and lay down in the grass.

"I'll catch up with you later," Roger called calmly. "I wanna see what happens."

I didn't even answer him I was running so fast. I ran so fast my feet almost slipped out from under me. I passed under the castle gates and Uno, Alex, and I cranked the wheel to close the gate.

"What should we do?" Alex yelled.

Uno had trouble talking. "We – we need to get Aunt Perrine."

"What?" Alex said. "What would she do?"

Uno began to run towards the house. "Come on," he yelled and we followed because we didn't know what else to do.

We ran into the living room and Uno pulled at a candle that was located beside the fireplace. Alex and I watched in amazement as a secret passage opened into a dark hall behind the fireplace. Uno ran in and we followed.

We ran down the long, stone hall. Candles on the wall lit up as if by magic, as we passed them. The hall ended at a spiral staircase that went up and down. We went up to a room, which seemed to be hidden in one of the back towers of the castle. It was circular and the window looked out on the old woods. Bookshelves, covered with ancient books, lined the walls, and there were glass cases filled with herbs, vials, and old skulls. Swords and axes were mounted to the walls next to cross bows and maces.

Alex and I stood staring out at the green bottles and ancient books. It looked like a wizard's study.

"What're you doing?" Uno called out. "We have to find the book."

"The what?" I asked stupidly.

"*Le Guide de Bagarreur Le Monstre*. I know she left it in here some place. If we can find it we won't have to tell Aunt Perrine and we won't get into trouble," Uno replied. "The book will tell us how to stop the zombies."

"Zombies?" Alex yelled.

"Book?" I said.

"Would you two stop staring and help me? We are going to be in so much trouble," Uno said.

I ran to the bookshelf and started reading the titles, "What does it look like?"

"It is quite large and bound in dragon skin." Aunt Perrine's voice caused us all stop dead in our tracks.

We turned to see her at the top of the stairs with her arms crossed angrily across her chest. She was wearing a robe with dragons embroidered on it and she looked fierce for an old lady. "I expected more of you, Uno. I expect Roger to be involved in zis kind of foolishness, but you are smarter zan zis."

Uno looked down. His red eyes filled with remorse and he looked a little sheepish.

"And you two boys," she said, "have gotten into nozing but trouble since you 'ave been 'ere."

"Sorry," Alex and I said in unison.

"Magic is dangerous. Little boys should not play wiz zings zey do not understand."

"Sorry," we said again.

"OK, zen. Now we deal wiz zeez zombies." Aunt Perrine looked around. "Where is Roger?"

"He stayed to watch the zombies," I said.

Aunt Perrine shook her head. "I'll deal with him later. But now, you three need weapons."

Alex and I just looked at each other.

Chapter 7

Three Easy Steps to Fighting Zombies

Aunt Perrine seemed very calm about everything. She hummed as she pulled a large, red book from the shelf. She set it down on the table. The book was bound in shiny, red scales and labeled in long elegant script, *Le Guide de Bagarreur Le Monstre.*

"What does it mean?" I asked Uno.

"It means the guidebook for monster fighters. It's *The Monster Hunter's Manual,*" Uno whispered.

Aunt Perrine took out the book and then walked over to a weapon-covered wall. She looked up at the swords, knives, crossbows, silver guns, crosses and shields. She shook her head, and turning away from the wall, went over to a chest.

"Ah," she said. "Zis is just what we need. Zee perfect weapon to fight zee zombies."

She pulled four out four very large, cartoon style hands, mounted on long, brightly colored plastic sticks. Each hand had one pointed finger. She put one stick in each of our hands and kept one for herself.

Alex looked at the stick. "You're joking right?"

"No. I never joke about zombies. Zey are very serious," she said in a tone that implied she might have been joking.

Alex opened his mouth to say something else, but Uno shook his head in warning and Alex shut his mouth.

"OK," she said. "Now we go to zee garage."

We left the secret tower and the secret hall and as we passed each candle, it mysteriously blew out again. Aunt Perrine closed the secret door and took us all to the garage. There we found five large refrigerators. Aunt Perrine opened one and looked at it.

"I need four buckets," she said.

The garage was a mess. There were piles of furniture, axes, books, and old clothes. All this junk was piled up in no particular order. It took us forever to find the buckets and then we placed them at Aunt Perrine's feet.

She handed us each a stack of brains, still in the wrapping from the supermarche. Uno started unwrapping the brains and putting them in his bucket and I figured I should follow his lead.

"I thought these were for us to eat," Alex said.

"No," Aunt Perrine said. "I 'ate brains. Do you like zem? I can save some for dinner tomorrow?"

"No! No! That's OK."

"So if you bought these two days ago and they are for the zombies," I said, "you must have known you were going to have to fight zombies this week?"

"You are a very smart boy." She unwrapped a brain and put it in the bucket. "Of course I know. You boys just lost your parents. I know zat you would try to zay goodbye to zem, so I buy brains, just in case."

"Oh," I said.

"That's really gross," Alex said.

"No more gross zan a 'ungry zombie."

"I get the brains," I said. "But what is this stick for."

"Zombies are easy to fight. Zere are zree steps. One...run...zey are very slow. Two...if zey get to close, push zem away with zis stick. Zree...give them a brain and zey go back to sleep."

"Really?" I asked.

"Really," Aunt Perrine said.

"OK," I said dropping my last brain in the bucket. "Let's go fight some zombies."

Aunt Perrine stood up. "Good for you. You say it like a real monster 'unter."

We all stood up, with a hand stick in one hand and a bucket of brains in the other. We must have looked ridiculous. We were two boys in pajamas, one cowardly vampire, and an old lady, but I knew in my heart we were warriors, and as we opened the gates to the castle, I prepared myself to fight like a lion.

I stepped out onto the cobblestoned road and prepared to face my worst fears. I took a deep breath and held my stick like a sword. The zombies oozy monsters stumbled up the road. The monsters were gross. They smelled like my brother's farts after he ate bean casserole, and looked like something I found on one of his old tissues, but as soon as I saw them stumbling and fumbling towards us, I knew there was nothing to be afraid of. They moaned and reached out for us, but they were so slow I could have outrun them without even running.

The first zombie came up to me with its hands outstretched. He kept bumping into things, and somehow I didn't feel too scared. It tried to grab me and I stepped aside. It fell. The next zombie came and I pushed it with my little stick. It fell too. I gave each fallen zombie a brain, they ate it hungrily and then dragged themselves up and stumbled back to the cemetery.

Alex looked as if he was having a lot of fun, as if he had discovered a new sport. He was jumping around the zombies, weaving in and out of them. He pushed them over and laughed at them. "You're a smelly, piece of dog fart," he said. "Take that, you gross zombie. You're so ugly that even other monsters won't hang out with you."

"Alex," Aunt Perrine scolded. "Don't taunt the zombies. Just give zem zee brains."

"Why not?" Alex pushed over another zombie. "It's not like it hurts their feeling or anything."

"Iz not nice," Aunt Perrine said. "Zey may have been someone nice in life."

Alex shrugged and started handing out brains. It kind of felt like Halloween, except the zombies never said trick or treat. Slowly, the zombies began to thin out. Every once in a while, Alex would softly say, "There you go, stinky," or "Have some brains, booger face." I tried to ignore him and focus on the zombies, but sometimes I had to laugh.

It wasn't until Uno started screaming that I felt a little jolt of fear, but when I turned around I saw that Roger was hanging around Uno's neck screaming, "Braiiiins. I want braiiiins!"

Uno pushed him off and Roger rolled around in the dirt laughing. "I got you good."

"If you're not going to be 'elpful," Aunt Perrine said. "Just go back to the castle."

Roger started hiking back up the hill to the castle, but he didn't make it. He fell and yelled out. I had just handed a zombie a brain and turned to see what was happening behind me. At first, I thought it was just another one of Roger's pranks. I shook my head and continued my work. Alex and Aunt Perrine obviously thought the same thing, but Roger's screams escalated and when I turned around again I noticed that there was something latched onto Roger's leg. It wasn't just Roger either. Some of the zombies appeared to be trapped as well.

"What's going on?" I asked. I stared at the field.

"Oh no!" Uno cried.

In the field in front of me, there were at least ten zombies in some kind of traps. They were groaning and thrashing, but they couldn't get out. Roger was caught too. He flailed helplessly in the grasp of a lock-jawed, silver trap.

For a minute, I panicked. I froze trying to figure out was going on. Alex, who never stopped to think about anything, ran blindly into the field after Roger. I looked around. Aunt Perrine was acting slowly, cautiously. She was looking through her bag, removing vials of colorful liquid.

"Ahhhhh!" Alex yelled as the jaws of a trap clamped over his leg. He couldn't move.

"What is it?" I asked Aunt Perrine.

"It's the slayers." She looked calm, but her jaw was set. She was ready to fight.

"What are slayers?" I asked.

"Not what, but who. They are men who think they are monster hunters."

"Think?"

Roger tried to pry the trap open on his leg and the trap tightened. It didn't just tighten, it got bigger and a part of it reached out to encompass Roger's other leg. Roger screamed and thrashed about desperately, but the more he fought the worse the trap became.

"We have to help them!" I cried.

I moved closer to the field, but stopped. I knew if I

stepped in, I would be trapped like the others.

"What should I do?" I asked Aunt Perrine.

Aunt Perrine lined the vials up in dirt in front of her.

"We wait," she said.

The minutes dragged by. Alex was yelling and struggling to escape. Roger was trying to pry the trap open with his bony fingers. The zombies moaned.

"Give the rest of the zombies their brains while we wait," Aunt Perrine told me.

I took her bucket and started handing out brains. Once fed, the zombies stopped wailing and sat down. Some of them even began digging back into the earth.

The slayers came from behind the castle. They looked like action heroes – James Bond on a mission. They were dressed all in black. Their hair was cut short and they wore bulletproof vests and combat boots. There were three of them and each of them held a machine gun in his hand.

The leader looked around and sized up the situation. "Bag what you can," the leader told the others.

The others each took one of the zombies and put it in a body bag while the leader walked up to Aunt Perrine. He was at least a foot taller than our tiny aunt, and he was young and in shape. Compared to him, she looked like the frailest old lady in the world.

"We just can't get away from you, can we, old lady?" he said.

"No," she answered plainly.

"I thought we told you to stay away so we can do our job."

"Zis is not your job. You are throwing the balance of ze world out of order."

"This is our job and you are in our way."

The other slayers began bagging another zombie and Roger began to scream. "Help me!" he yelled. "Don't let them take me!"

"Help him," I said in desperation.

"There's no help for monsters, boy," the leader said to me. "There's no place in this world for things like him."

"We'll be taking that one too," the leader said, pointing to Uno.

Uno hid behind Aunt Perrine, but Aunt Perrine only smiled and shook her head. "When will you learn?" she said. With that, she crushed all of the vials she had laid on the ground. The liquids blended together and formed a green fog. The fog rose up in twisting, spirals like serpents crawling towards heaven. It rose up and then spread out over the field. It engulfed Aunt Perrine until she was lost in it and I could hardly see her face. She raised her right arm and the traps opened. Roger ran towards the castle as soon as he was free. Aunt Perrine raised her left hand and the soldier's guns turned to smoke and vanished in their hands.

The leader looked angry, but not surprised. Uno ran off toward the castle behind Roger.

"Why'd you do that, old lady?" the leader asked. "Why do you always protect the monsters?"

"You and I 'ave a different idea of what a monster is," she said.

Aunt Perrine looked tired, as if the spell had taken all her energy. I ran to her side and held her up. "Zanks you," she said.

"Someday you won't have all your tricks," the leader said. "And then it'll be you who loses."

Aunt Perrine just shook her head. Alex ran to her and she wrapped her free arm around He hugged her.

"Bonsoir," Aunt Perrine said.

Alex and I helped her climb up the hill and into the castle. The slayers took the two zombies they had captured, put them in a black van and drove away.

"Those poor creatures," Aunt Perrine said as we closed the castle gates and I wasn't entirely sure if she was talking about the zombies or the slayers.

We helped Aunt Perrine into the house and she sat down on the chair. She looked very tired, but she still gave us her usual warm smile. I fetched Aunt Perrine some tea and she took her time sipping it. It wasn't long before the color returned to her face.

"I'm getting old," she said. "I'm not as strong as I used to be."

"You were amazing," I said.

"Zanks you."

Alex's smile covered his entire face. "That smoke was awesome," Alex commented.

Aunt Perrine took another sip of tea. "Zanks you," she said again.

"Thank *you* for helping us," I said.

"You should be more careful next time."

Alex and I both rushed to promise that we would never make that mistake again. We would never use magic we didn't understand. Aunt Perrine took our promises as earnest.

"I think I should rest now," she said and she pulled herself up out of her chair and went into her room. She closed the door and Alex and I were left alone with our thoughts. As we left the living room, I couldn't help but notice that she had left *The Monster Hunter's Manual* on the coffee table.

Chapter 8

Ms. Angerboda

After Aunt Perrine had drifted off to sleep, Alex and I went to check on Uno and Roger. Roger was sitting alone in his bed. He was crying.

"What happened?" I asked.

Roger shook his head. "Uno hasn't come back."

"What!" Alex exclaimed.

"Uno never came back," Roger repeated.

"We need to tell Aunt Perrine," I said.

Roger shook his head mournfully. "We can't."

"Why not?" Alex asked.

"Because, she made a deal."

"What deal!" I asked.

"About a year ago she saved both of us from the slayers. She saved us by sneaking in and stealing us from them in the middle of the night. The slayers were angry and they came to the village to find us. There were hundreds of them and they had big guns and helicopters. Aunt Perrine made a deal with them. They said she could have us just once, but if she ever stole from them again, it would be war. She promised. She won't go back on a promise."

"But this is different!" I exclaimed. "She would never let those creeps have Uno."

"She's just one woman," Roger said.

"You saw her," I said. "She's more than that."

Roger just shook his head. "She won't risk fighting them all for him. She can't. There are just too many of them."

"OK. Then we should go get him ourselves," Alex said.

"How?" I asked.

A cheeky look appeared in Alex's eyes. "She left the book

on the coffee table. We could just borrow it."

"I don't know," I said.

"Are you really going to let those jerks take Uno?"

"No," I said. "Let's go get it."

Aunt Perrine was sound asleep by the time we crept down the stairs. It was easy to slide the book off the table and make it outside into the courtyard. The book was enormous. It was so thick and heavy it took two of us to carry it out there. The three of us sat down in the courtyard with the flashlight surrounded by cats. We looked at the book. It had thousands of pages all written in French.

"I can't read any of this," I said.

I passed the book to Roger. He flipped through the pages. "What am I looking for?"

"A spell to help us find him," I answered. "And get him back."

"So maybe teleportation?" Roger suggested.

"Maybe."

Roger flipped the pages. The book was beautiful. It was handwritten and illuminated. Letters were drawn to look like animals, and there were pictures embossed with gold. There were illustrations of monsters I had never heard of or seen before, along with enormous creatures with tentacles and scales, shark men, and demons. Occasionally there was a feather or a scale glued to the paper. There were old notes carefully tucked into pockets. Samples of flowers and herbs were glued next to detailed drawings of plants and animals. Each page offered some new beauty, but it was impossible for me to make any sense of it.

"I can't find anything," Roger said.

"Keep looking," I urged.

Roger flipped through more pages, the pictures and the handwriting changed. There were now herbs, wands and fairies. Each page was more beautiful than the next, but there was nothing that seemed to be able to help us. The book just went on and on. It would take forever to find what we were looking for.

I didn't see Eleanor sneak up behind us, but her voice made me look up from the book.

"How did you get that?" she whispered. "Lady Perrine will kill you."

"The slayers got Uno," I said.

"What? How?"

"We don't know," Alex said. "But we have to help him."

Eleanor reached out and took the book. "Well you're never going to find a spell to find him in the section on botany." She flipped through a few pages and found the spell she was looking for. The page she stopped on had a picture of a circle with an object in the center of it. "This is a spell that can transport us to the location of any person in the world. I think this is what we need."

We all nodded in agreement.

Suddenly Eleanor looked at each of with a seriousness that made me shudder. "You know that if they catch us, they'll never let us go."

We all nodded.

"Do you still have the amulet the Moleman gave you?" she asked.

I was astonished. "How did you know about that?"

"They told me. They think you are going to be the next monster hunter. The amulet they gave you is the amulet of the hunter. They make a new one for each new hunter and give the amulet the power to bring its wearer, and all who are touching him, back to Chateau Larcher. You are wearing the key to our escape. Don't lose it. I'll get us there, but only the amulet can return us."

"I won't lose it," I said.

Eleanor searched around. "We need something that

belongs to Uno for the teleportation spell."

Roger took out an old teddy bear and handed it to Eleanor. She took it and placed it on the ground. She drew a circle in the dirt around the bear.

"Whatever happens, we have to stay together," she said.

We all nodded. Eleanor took our hands, and Alex and I took Roger's hand. We formed a circle around the bear. Eleanor spoke in French. The words came out clearly. I closed my eyes and when I opened them, we were in the dark. Alex's grip tightened in mine and I could hear his breathing increase. He was afraid and so was I. I wished we were back in the cemetery with the zombies.

Something moaned in the darkness and Eleanor appeared. She lit up like a candle in the dark illuminating the room we were in. I bit my lip to prevent myself from screaming. The room was filled with monsters. There were zombies, werewolves and horned demons. They moaned and snarled, but it didn't matter because they were all caged and tied down.

"Stay here," Eleanor whispered. "I'll find Uno."

Eleanor vanished and left us in the dark to listen to the snarling of the hundreds of unhappy monsters that surrounded us. It seemed to take forever. We stood perfectly still holding each other's hands in the dark. We were afraid that if we moved we would seen.

A light switched on in a room at the end of the hall and we all dropped to the cool ground. We tried to make ourselves invisible. We could hear footsteps coming closer and voices. My heart was pounding in my ears. I couldn't breathe. I pulled Alex close to me. The footsteps came closer and I could hear the slayers talking. They were talking in English.

"We should just kill the old lady," a man said.

"That's not what Ms. Angerboda wants," a woman

responded. Her voice was cold. So cold, I shivered.

"I don't see the point in keeping her alive."

"It's not your job to understand. You aren't important. You do what you are told to do. You capture everything you can and not just the monsters. All of them. Ms. Angerboda particularly wants the mole people that live beneath the castle," the woman said. "And she wants the girl, the ghost child."

The man seemed irritated by this. "Why? They are harmless."

"What did I tell you about asking questions?" The woman's voice was so icy it sent chills down my spine.

"I'll do my best. The castle is well guarded. There is a line that we can't cross. The old lady is powerful."

"Do your best. You are a resourceful man. Maybe you can find a way to lure them away from the castle…"

The voices faded and the footsteps vanished. I realized I had been holding my breath and I summoned the courage to breath. Alex breathed in deeply to. It was only when the light went out and the footsteps completely disappeared that I found the courage to speak.

"We have to get out of here," I whispered.

Eleanor appeared again and the darkness vanished with her. "I found him," she said.

We all followed her through an ocean of howling monsters to where Alex sat, weeping in a cage. I reached through the bars and took his hands. He smiled up at me. Everyone huddled around me and I put my arms around my little group of friends.

"Chateau Larcher," I said clearly, and before the words had even left my mouth, we were home. I exhaled. We were back and we were safe.

Uno wrapped his arms around me. "Thank you."

"We would never leave you," I said.

The five of us climbed up to Eleanor's room and sat on the floor with the book between us. I looked at Eleanor. "No more lies. What's going on here?"

"I shouldn't tell," Eleanor protested.

"You have to. We have to know," I said.

Eleanor nodded and her light faded a little, as if her sorrow dimmed her very existence. "Every thousand years a new monster hunter is born. It is up to the old hunter to find the new hunter. When the new monster hunter comes of age and is fully trained, the old monster hunter will die. It is at that time that Angerboda will break free from her prison. The new monster hunter must fight and imprison her again or she will rule the world and monsters will take over the world. If they are working for Angerboda, something has gone wrong. She shouldn't be able to influence the outside world. Aunt Perrine used powerful magic to bind her to the earth a thousand years ago. The magic shouldn't be fading yet."

"So Aunt Perrine is a thousand years old?" Alex asked.

"Older," Eleanor said. "She's been a hunter for a thousand years. She's been alive for longer."

"Wow."

"She thinks one of you will be the next hunter. So do the molemen."

Alex looked at me with envy. He knew that they had given me the amulet because they thought I would be the hunter. I saw his look. He wanted to be a hunter too. I clutched the amulet. I could already see it dividing us.

"Only one of us?" I asked.

"Only one of you."

"If she's a hunter, why does she keep so many monsters?" Alex asked with a hint of bitterness.

Eleanor threw up her hands in frustration. "Because, the monster hunter is more than a killer. She's not a slayer. It is her job to keep balance, to protect the innocent no matter who they are. In the old days, in the Dark Ages, there were monsters everywhere. People lived in fear because the last hunter didn't do his job, but Aunt Perrine changed that, she knows the balance. She's made her mistakes, but she keeps the world safe."

Uno looked confused. "How do you know all this?"

Eleanor hesitated. She was afraid to say what she needed to say. I smiled at her and she smiled back. "I'm her daughter."

We were all silent for a moment. Eleanor's light faded and shadow passed over the room. I could hardly see her face. Her glow was a pale blue in the moonlight.

"When we were alone in that room," Roger asked. "We heard some people talking about a Ms. Angerboda. Could that be Angerboda?"

"No. It hasn't been a thousand years yet," Eleanor said. "She shouldn't be free yet."

"The old ones said that too," I said. "They said Angerboda walks again."

No one answered me. There was only silence.

"We need to tell Aunt Perrine about this," I continued. "This is important."

"She'll be mad," Roger said.

"Who cares? She needs to know."

Everyone followed me back into the house. I hesitated before I knocked on her door. My knock was met by silence. I knocked again and the door opened. Aunt Perrine came out in her long bathrobe. She turned on the light and invited us in.

"Please sit," she said.

We all found places to sit amidst the army of cats that covered her bed and sofa. Aunt Perrine sat down in a large armchair and studied our faces. In that light, surrounded by her cats, she looked almost fearsome and I couldn't summon the courage to talk. "So," she said. "You all 'ave gotten into to trouble again. Twice in one night?"

I nodded. "We need to tell you something."

"Yes."

"We took your book." I handed it back to her. She took the book and looked at me with an almost angry expression.

"And?" she said.

Alex stood up. "The slayers took Uno and we all went to save him and we heard some people saying that Ms. Angerboda wants to catch the molemen and Eleanor." He blurted the words out so fast I almost didn't understand him. He sat back down.

"And," Eleanor added, "the old ones said that Angerboda walks again."

Aunt Perrine was quiet. She leaned back in her chair and stroked the small tabby cat that had curled up on her lap.

"So zis is all?" she asked after a while.

"Yes," we all answered in unison.

"Well," she said calmly. "I'll take care of it."

She picked up a bowl of candies and handed one to everyone but Eleanor. We each took one and put it in our mouths. Just like my first night at the castle, I found myself overwhelmed by the desire to sleep.

"Now off to bed," Aunt Perrine ordered. We all listened except Eleanor who curled up in her mother's bed. I climbed the stairs and fell into my bed. Alex collapsed next to me.

"Can I sleep with you?"

"Yes," I said, and I drifted off into a deep, dreamless sleep.

Chapter 9

The Old Cathedral

We all slept late and Roger and Uno slept through the day. When Alex and I woke, Aunt Perrine made us a brunch of different kinds of crepe filled with everything imaginable. It was like the night before had never happened. Aunt Perrine didn't mention it. She hummed happily, as she always did, and set us down to practice our French.

In the afternoon, she took us into the village and introduced us to our neighbors. We met a nice lady and her two little girls, an old farmer who lived mostly with his pigs, a heavy lady who was the school teacher, a priest, the lady who owned the local creperie, and an artist. Of course, we couldn't talk to any of them because we still didn't speak French, but that didn't stop any of them from talking to us in rapid French like we should understand them.

We went to the boulangerie to get bread and pastries stuffed with meat and ham and to the patisserie to get sweet pastries and tarts. For dinner, we ate at the creperie. Aunt Perrine bought us each a little knight from the toy store and some new shirts. By the end of the day, we were tired and had almost forgotten all the adventures of the night.

We didn't talk about what happened, we just enjoyed being out and part of the village. I listened to the French and tried to understand as much as I could and Alex tried to communicate with the village children by grunting at them and poking them. The children may not have understood him, but he certainly made them laugh.

Evening came quickly and we were both more than happy to go to bed early. As usual, Aunt Perrine came upstairs and sat on Alex's bed. I lay down next to him and she told us a story.

"*Once upon a time,*" she began. For the first time, I realized her accent faded when she told stories and her English became clear and crisp, as if she was born to it.

"*There was a poor serf.* Do you know what a serf is?"

Alex shook his head.

"In the Middle Ages, they were the poor people that were bound to the land and almost slaves to the lords of castles like this one. *So, there was a poor serf girl. The girl was no prettier than any other and she wasn't a hard worker so her poor parents thought that she was doomed to be a spinster with no dowry. The girl had nothing, but one day, a Peluda came to the village. A Peluda is a horrible dragon with a porcupine-like body and a mess of hair-like projections hanging from its body that are covered in poison. He could launch these at will, killing the person who had been shot. The Peluda terrorized the village for over a year and the people sought help from the lord of the land. The sought him because it was said that he was the keeper of the old magic and that he would know what to do.*

"*But the lord was old and he was not strong enough to defeat the Peluda himself. So the lord of the land decided to make a sacrifice to the Peluda. He would offer it a young girl and since the poor serf girl had no money, prospects or particular beauty, she was chosen to be given to the monster.*

"*Now the girl was terrified, but she was also quite clever and she knew the secret ways of magic, so the night before she was to be given to the beast, she went into the woods and found the old ones. She begged for their help and since she had always honored them and kept their shrines, they helped her.*

"*The old ones gave the girl three rings and said she must rub them in times of need.*

"*The next day the lord of the land ordered the girl to be dressed in rich velvet and fine jewels and had her tied to a tree* for the Peluda. The Peluda came and carried her away to his cave.

"'I would like to eat you,' the Peluda said. 'For I am very hungry.'

"'Let me sing to you first,' the girl said. And the girl had a lovely voice and the Peluda smiled as she sang to him. He became comfortable and while she sang the girl rubbed the first ring.

"The Peluda cried out, for it had become blind. Enraged, it shot its arrows blindly into the cave and sought the girl out, but the girl was not afraid and she rubbed the second ring. This ring made the Peluda deaf and the Peluda fell to its knees and wept. When the girl rubbed the third ring,it became a sword. It was common knowledge in those days that Peluda's only vulnerable spot was his tail, and the girl cut off his tail, killing the beast."

"The girl was celebrated as a hero and the lord called her to the castle. The lord was a wise man who was known throughout the kingdom for his justice and virtue. He took the girl aside and gave her two choices. He said she had earned a great prize. He said he would give her great wealth and land that she and her family could keep as her own. She would never want for anything again or she could choose to marry his son, the heir to his land and fiefdom. His son was a bit of a dimwit and she would have to rule for him, but she would inherit the lord's strength and power and a book of magic that contained all the secrets of all the monsters in the world. She would be given the power to protect the kingdom from monsters, as he had once done in his youth."

"What do you think the girl chose," Aunt Perrine asked me.

"She chose the magic," I said.

"Yes. She chose the magic, because although the girl seemed plain, she had a warrior's heart and sometimes it doesn't matter at all what something seems to be, only what it is. The lord knew this and that is why, when the lord died, the girl ruled over all vast lands and inherited all his wisdom and power."

For once, Alex had listened. He had sat up and really listened.

"Do you like my story?" Aunt Perrine asked.

"It's my favorite so far," I answered.

"Mine too," she said. "It is time to sleep now, little princes, and dream of magic castles and secret caverns."

We both nodded and went to sleep. We ignored the rattling and bumping from the attic. It's funny how something that once seemed so scary can become kind of reassuring. It was nice to think that Roger and Uno were upstairs rattling around. It made the old castle seem more like a home, filled with people you liked. I slept better that night than any other night since I had left America.

In the morning, Alex went out with Roger. Roger said he knew these gnomes who lived in an enchanted forest. He said that the gnomes could find mushrooms that would make you taller and shorter. Alex, like a boy reading *Alice in Wonderland*, was completely fascinated.

I let Alex go. I stayed and studied French with Aunt Perrine. She sat with me, helped me with my work, and spoke to me in words I could understand.

Alex told me I was crazy to spend my day with an old lady when I could be finding gnomes with a walking skeleton, but I knew that I had chosen more wisely. I had seen Aunt Perrine fight the slayers. I knew that if I really ever wanted to be the monster hunter, I should stay close to her. And from the first moment I knew there were monster hunters, I knew I wanted to be one.

Alex came back for lunch and we all ate outside.

"You should stay and practice your French," Aunt Perrine said to him patiently.

"Roger says we can go back to the gnomes this afternoon. You would like them Gabriel," Alex said. "They live in little cities in mushroom houses and have crickets for pets, like dogs."

I shook my head. "You can show me some other time. I want to stay with Aunt Perrine."

"Come on," Alex begged. "You'd really like it. They make honey wine and candied grapes."

"You have Roger," I said.

"Yeah," Alex said in a forlorn voice.

After lunch, Alex ran off into the woods with Roger and I sat at the table with Aunt Perrine.

"Do you really want to work all day?" she asked.

I shook my head.

"Would you like me to show you the most magical place in the castle?"

I nodded and smiled broadly.

She took my hand and we walked out of our little house and into the courtyard. It was a quiet afternoon. There was no sound in the courtyard except the rustling of leaves and the purring of sleeping cats.

We walked slowly across the courtyard to the great church, Aunt Perrine unlocked the doors and we walked in. The church was stunning. The ceilings were so high they seemed to float above me and were supported by a series of long slender columns that had reliefs of monsters and dragons chasing people. Some of the monsters were even eating people. The monsters decorated every column, every corner. They were everywhere and the engravings had been painted in bright reds and yellows so the monsters seemed to leap off the walls. Along the top of the columns, above the monsters, there were engravings of saints and angels and Jesus and Mary as if to say those things were somehow above those of us who lived below, with the monsters.

The walls were made of stone, stacked up and smoothed over. There weren't many windows and the ones there were seemed not to fit. They seemed wrong in the ancient church.

"The church was built first," Aunt Perrine said. "It was built in the year 900, when most of the land was still building with wood. They built it here because this place was and had always been sacred. The Romans built here, the Celts, everyone. It wasn't until a hundred years later that they tore down the wood fortress and built the church into the stone castle."

"Why would they have all these horrible pictures in a church?" I asked.

"All the really old churches have them," Aunt Perrine said. "The one at Chauvigny has the same pictures. I think that's just the way life was back then. People lived in constant fear. There were monsters everywhere. The monsters didn't have to hide. They roamed the hills and hunted in villages. It's better now and most people have forgotten that there ever were monsters, but these churches serve to remind us of the way things were."

"Why do the windows look so weird?"

"All the original stained glass was blown out in the Second World War. These are just cheap copies. It happened to many of them, all over the Loire Valley. "

"Aunt Perrine?" I asked.

"Yes," she said.

"Can I help you?"

"With what?"

"I want to be the next monster hunter," I said. "I want to learn from you."

Aunt Perrine only smiled the smile that adults smile when they don't want to answer your questions. "Let's light candles for your parents."

We went to the knave of the church and lit two candles. Aunt Perrine knelt in front of the candles and she said two prayers, one for my mom and one for my dad. The church bells above us struck three and the priest came in to prepare for a service.

"It's still used?" I asked.

"Oh yes," she answered. "In a few hours zis place will be filled with people."

"Why is this place the most magic place in the castle?" I asked.

She put her hand on my shoulder and closed her eyes. The stained glass bathed her in an eerie blue light.

"Can't you feel it," she said.

I shook my head.

"This place is the source of my magic."

"I don't understand."

"Give it time," she said. "Some magic takes time."

I looked around at all the strange monsters. Two-headed monsters with beaks carrying people away. Baby-faced monsters with lizard like bodies. I thought it must have been terrifying to live back then, to be afraid all the time. Suddenly, I thought of Eleanor, all alone in her tower and I wondered if she had been afraid.

"You know," Aunt Perrine said. "Zere is more to being a monster 'unting than 'unting and fighting."

"What else is there?" I asked.

"We must also keep the world safe. Zere are bad monsters and zere are good monsters. We must protect those that need protecting."

"Like Roger and Uno? Like the Molemen?"

"Yes, and zere is more." Aunt Perrine's voice took on a sorrowful tone. "Zere is a price that comes with it. Your fazer once zought he wanted to be the next 'unter, but then he fell in love and had you. It is a hard path."

"I think I understand…" I interrupted. "You've been here for a long time and you lost your daughter."

Aunt Perrine looked off into the distance. Her eyes filled with tears. "Yes," she said. "Zere are some zings I would change, but for me zere can be no ozer life. It is my destiny. Is it your destiny, little prince?"

I nodded. "I think it is."

"You cannot zink. You must know in your 'eart. If you choose zis path you will fight unspeakable evil. You vill do battle to protect zis world. You 'ave 'eard much of zis Angerboda. All ze monsters and spirits 'ave whispered of her. You 'ave 'eard 'er name in all your adventures. You know she is coming and you know she vill try to kill you and all zose you love. *If* you are ze next monster hunter, you and you alone, must face 'er in the end. I cannot fight Angerboda again. If I did zis, we would all die and she would be freed. I must train you and teach you and when you are ready, I must let go of the magic that has kept me in this world so very long. When I am gone, you vill 'ave to fight the mother of all monsters, as I once did and as the 'unter before me did. So, little prince, is it your destiny?"

"It is," I said. "I know it is. This is why all these horrible things have happened, because I was meant to be here."

"What about your brozer?"

"He's fine," I said dismissively.

"Yes," Aunt Perrine said. "I will teach you to be a monster 'unter, but first you must do something for me."

I nodded eagerly. "OK."

"I have a mission for you." Aunt Perrine put her hand on my shoulder. "Go and find your brother. You will need 'im. Take 'im and go see the troll under zee bridge in zee village. Ask the troll three questions. 'What do you do with your days?' 'Where do you come from?' And 'What's most important to you?' And zen go and ask the man who lives on the farm on the way to the dolmen the same question. Come back and tell me what you have learned."

I nodded. "Is that all?"

"For now," Aunt Perrine said.

I sprinted away from the church and breakneck speed. I didn't know how to get to the gnomes so I ran upstairs and went into the attic. I shook Uno's coffin. I shook it so violently that it almost tipped over. Uno came out.

"What?" he said crabbily.

"I need to find the gnome's kingdom!"

"Why?"

"I have a mission."

"I'm sleeping." Uno began to pull his coffin shut.

"Just tell me how to get there?"

"All right." He drew me a map with crayon and construction paper.

I set out into the woods alone. It didn't take me long to regret my decision.

Once you know that there are monsters and ghosts and things that go bump in the night, it's harder to convince yourself there's nothing to be afraid of. The woods around Chateau Larcher were old and the trees were tall. The wind whistled through the branches making them moan and I couldn't help but shudder.

In the distance, I could hear a low snarl and I froze.

"Alex!" I called my brother's name and looked down at Uno's crudely drawn map.

"Alex!" I called again.

I began to walk more quickly in the direction I thought I was supposed to be going, but the further I walked the more I realized I was completely lost. I looked at the map. It was terrible, nonsensical. *Turn left at the large, knotted tree.* All the trees had knots. What was that supposed to mean?

"Alex!" My cry was becoming desperate.

Turn right at large, moss-covered rock. I looked around.

94

There were rocks of various sizes scattered throughout the woods. I yelled and ripped up the map in moment of utter frustration, and then panicking, I tried to pick up the pieces. A gentle breeze came and the pieces slipped through my fingers. The map vanished into thin air and I was left alone and lost.

I heard the snarl again and tried to remain as calm as I could.

Suddenly, something or things jumped out at me from the woods and pinned me to ground.

I screamed. Alex and Roger rolled off me in hysterical laughter.

"You were so scared," Alex laughed.

"I was not!" I argued. "I was just lost.

"No," Roger said. "We completely had you. We got you good."

"You did not."

"Did so," Alex said.

"Did not."

"Did so," Alex said more firmly.

"OK," I admitted. "Maybe just a little."

Alex smiled and helped me to my feet. "You wanna meet the gnomes?"

"No, I'm on an important mission," I said.

"What mission?"

"Aunt Perrine sent me on a mission to meet a troll and she wants you to help me," I said.

"Are you sure you don't want to meet the gnomes?"

"Yes. We have a mission."

"Why are we on a mission?"

I hesitated. I didn't want to tell him the truth. I didn't want him to know I wanted to be the next hunter, because I thought that he might want to be the hunter to. I didn't want to have to fight with him over it. I struggled to find a lie, but the words got stuck in my mouth. I didn't want to lie to Alex any more than I wanted to tell him about the origin of my mission.

"If you're not going to tell me," Alex said. "I'm going back to the gnomes."

I needed Alex. I couldn't let him go back. "I asked Aunt Perrine if I could be the next monster hunter."

"You did?"

"I did."

"But," Alex said, "what about me?"

"You can be my assistant."

"So you get to live forever and learn magic and fight dragons, and I get to sit at home and polish your boots?" Alex said with bitterness.

"No, I didn't mean it like that."

"You want to leave me behind."

His voice was so filled with sadness that I almost changed my mind, almost turned around and handed Alex the amulet, but I couldn't do it. All my life I had dreamt and read of magic and dragons. I had spent a lot of time buried in books and movies. This was everything I had ever wanted and I couldn't give it up, not for Alex, not for anyone.

"No," I said. "But it has to be one of us, doesn't it? And the molemen gave me the amulet. It has to be me."

"Why should I help you?"

"Because I'm your brother."

"OK," Alex said after a while. "I'll help. What do you have to do?"

"We have to go see the troll under the bridge."

"She wants us to go see that troll under the bridge?" Roger repeated.

"Yeah," I said.

"She must think you're a hunter already if she wants you

to go see that rotten old lump," Roger said.

Roger led the way and we all followed him. It was a short walk. Alex and Roger talked all the way there. They told me everything I ever wanted to know and more about the gnomes. It didn't sound too interesting to me but they seemed to think it was fascinating.

I nodded politely, but I wasn't listening. Nothing they said mattered. My mind was fixed on one thing, the *Monster Hunter's Manual* and all the magic that lay inside.

Chapter 10

The Farmer and the Troll

By the time we made it to the bridge, evening was coming. The bridge was cramped and aging. It was hardly large enough for one car to drive over. It was made of stone and it passed over a slow, muddy river.

"This is it," Roger said.

I looked at the muddy embankment with trepidation, but Roger slid down through the mud without thinking twice. He hit the bottom and signaled for us to follow. I watched Alex slide through the mud and then followed them. The bank was wet and I sank into the dirt at the bottom. My shoes were sloshy with dirt and water. The mud didn't faze Roger or Alex who were splashing in it and throwing mud clods at each other, but I didn't like being knee deep in muck.

"So where's the troll?" I asked Roger.

Roger smiled. He looked at the embankment beneath the bridge and found an odd green stone.

"It's a troll stone," Roger said. He pulled the stone out of the mud and pushed it back in. "Trolls like the mud."

An eerie green light spread out by the troll stone and formed a rectangle. The rectangle became a door. Roger knocked three times and the door opened.

The troll wasn't what I expected. He looked old and bent. He was big and ugly. He had a huge nose and beady, black eyes that peered out at me from his hairy, sloped brow. There was moss on his back and in between his huge, muddy toes. He had warts on his nose and the parts of him that weren't covered in hair were covered in moss. He wasn't as big as I expected and didn't stand much taller than a man, but his shoulder's were broad and he was as wide as an aging oak.

"H-hello," I said with a stutter. "The Lady Perrine sent us."

The troll growled unhappily.

"She wanted me to ask some questions."

The troll growled again and I backed up into the mud.

"This is a cool house," Alex said peering inside. "Do you have trees growing in there? How did you get trees in there?"

The troll stared at Alex and then his face softened a little. He spoke slowly with a thick French accent. "I work at night," he said. "You people think you can only build by destroying. We trolls know that the best building is by preserving. I carefully dug up the roots and carried the tree down here. It holds up the walls. If you look up on the street, you can see the leaves."

Alex ran through the mud and looked up. "That's awesome," he said. "I'm Alex and that's Roger." He pointed to Roger, who was building some kind of sculpture out of the mud. "And that's Gabe."

"Come in then," the troll said gruffly, and we all followed him into his house.

The troll's house was built out of rock and trees. The roots of the trees above were woven together to form the walls. The parts of the walls that weren't supported by the roots were supported by stone. Small trees grew up from the ground and their branches stretched up to the ceiling supporting the roof of the house and covering it in a blanket of green leaves. Small colored stones littered the mud and rock floor. There was a rock table and bed, and there were leaves everywhere. Pictures of other trolls hung on the carved walls. Generations of trolls lined the walls.

The troll sat down on a stone stool and glared at me from across the room. I shuffled uncomfortably, trying to summon the courage to ask him the questions I had come to ask.

Alex sat down on the floor across from the troll and smiled vibrantly. "I met the gnomes today."

"You met Gnilkolay?" the troll asked in his gruff voice.

"Yes," Alex said with a smile. "He taught me how to make tea with mushrooms."

"Gnome tea is a fine delicacy," the troll said. "I am Lore. I would like to try some of this tea."

Alex stood up. "Do you have a pot?"

Lore took a teapot that had been hanging off a branch down from the ceiling and handed it to my brother. The pot, carved from stone, had runes engraved around its base. Lore started a fire and my brother went outside to gather mushrooms and water. I sat quietly and waited for my chance to speak.

It wasn't long before Lore had made a pleasant fire that crackled and sputtered. Alex came back and put the water and mushrooms in the pot. He placed the pot over the fire and we all waited for the water to boil.

Roger stood up and smelled the tea. He smiled at Lore.

Lore grimaced. "You are the undead?"

"Kind of."

"I hear it is a hard existence, being undead."

Roger nodded. "It is."

"I offer you my sympathy," Lore said earnestly.

"Thank you."

"The tea should ease your suffering," Lore continued. "Gnome tea is supposed to take away all suffering."

The water boiled and the teapot cried out. Lore put out four cups on his table and Alex took the pot off the fire. He filled each cup carefully. The steamy mixture smelled like cloves and cinnamon. I picked up my cup. The tea was red, like fire. Steam curled up and over the cup. I sipped it gently, careful not to burn my lips. The hot liquid was bitter, but strangely soothing. I leaned back in the stone chair and closed my eyes.

"It is delicious," Lore said.

Alex smiled. "Thank you."

We all drank deeply and there was a moment of contented silence. We all sat sipping our tea and contemplating the brilliance of the gnomes. Even Lore smiled a little over his teacup.

"So," Lore said after a time. "You are Lady Perrine's new protégé."

"I am," I answered.

"I do not look forward to her passing. She has been kind to us."

"Can I ask you a question?" I asked hesitantly.

"What?" Lore asked.

"Where do you come from?"

"I come from here," he said. "I've always been here. I was born here. I raised my children here. My mother," he pointed to one of the trolls on the wall, "came here with the Vikings. My people are from the North."

"What's most important to you," I pressed.

Lore's frown deepened. "My family, my home, the earth."

"What do you do with your days?" I continued.

Lore snarled again and I set down my tea.

Roger laughed at me. "Don't mind him He doesn't understand. He doesn't mean to be rude. He's only a person."

Lore looked at me with an angry glare. I had clearly offended him, but I wasn't sure how.

"You are supposed to offer him something," Roger whispered in my ear. "He invited you into his home. Alex gave him the tea. You have to give him something as well."

"Oh," I said. I thought for a moment and then I began to dig through my pockets.

"I thank you for inviting me into your wonderful home," I said. "And I would like to offer you..."

I didn't have much in my pockets, just a few coins, some old gum, and one the knights Aunt Perrine had given me. I took out the knight and handed it to Lore with the coins.

Lore took the quarter and smiled. "I have never seen an American coin before. I've only seen them in books," he said. "I spend my days with my family when they are here and resting when they are not. My time grows thin. I am not as young as I used to be."

"Thank you." I gave Lore a dime and a nickel. He seemed pleased, but snarled at me, for good measure, one last time, before showing me to the door.

On the way out, Lore hesitated. "How is Lady Perrine?"

"Fine."

"Tell her to visit sometime. There aren't many of us left that remember the good times. The old times. She should come."

I nodded earnestly. "I'll tell her."

"Thank you for showing us your house," Alex said. "I loved your trees."

Lore smiled at Alex, which was a fearsome sight, but somehow I was a little jealous that he hadn't smiled at me.

The three of us had to scramble to pull our way out of the muddy ditch beneath the bridge. It was much easier sliding down the mud than climbing out of it. By the time we pulled ourselves to the road, we were all covered from head to toe in mud. Roger was so caked in filth that I could barely see the white of his bones.

"There's one more person to see," I said.

"Who?" Alex asked.

"A man on a farm."

"I can't go," Roger said.

"Really?" Alex said this with obvious disappointment.

"Look at me." Roger pointed to his bony body. "I can't walk around in the world of men. I can't be seen."

"You've been walking around all day," Alex said.

"In the shadow, but I can't go knock on some farmer's door."

"I won't go if Roger can't go."

"No," Roger said. "Go ahead. I'll go bother Uno. You

two have fun."

We waved goodbye and started down the long road of men.

"Does the farmer speak English?" Alex asked.

"I guess. Why would Aunt Perrine send me to see someone who didn't?"

Alex shrugged and walked behind me kicking the dirt. The sun was beginning to set casting long shadows on the road. The farmer's house wasn't far. It was a small, old house. It was surrounded by fields of sunflowers. Alex and I walked slowly up the drive and knocked on the door. The old man that answered the door had a cigarette hanging from his mouth.

"Quoi?" he said.

"Bonjour," I said.

"Quoi?" he said again.

"Parlez-vous Anglais? Do you speak English?"

"Yes. What do you want?"

The man seemed angry and he smelled worse than the troll. I opened my mouth to speak, but couldn't find the words so I just stood there with my mouth hanging open. Alex also looked like a deer caught in the headlights and seemed much more afraid of the old man than the zombies from the other night. The old man just continued glaring at us. I finally mustered the strength to speak. "Madame Perrine sent us to see you."

"I don't like Madame Perrine," he said.

"She wanted me to ask you some questions."

"Tell that old bag to get lost," he said. "I got nothing to say to her or any of her family."

"Please, sir," I persisted.

He relented. "What questions?"

"Where do you come from?" I said.

"None of your business."

"What's most important to you?"

"My privacy, now get lost."

He slammed the door in our faces, and Alex and I were left with our mouths hanging open.

"Should we knock again? "Alex asked.

I knocked again.

"Go away!"a voice called from behind the door. "I have a shot gun and I'll fill your back ends with lead if you don't clear off."

That was all it took. Alex and I ran back to the road as fast as we could. We scampered down the road like children that had just gotten into some kind of trouble and didn't want to be caught. It was dark by the time we made it back to the village. Everything was quiet and our muddy, sneakers squeaked on the cobblestone road. As we walked back to the castle, I tried to think of what I had learned from the farmer and the troll. I tried to put together some story that I could tell Aunt Perrine to make her think I would be the perfect monster hunter.

The only thing I had learned was that Alex was all I had left. He had helped me at every turn. I put my hand on Alex's shoulder as we walked down the road.

"Thank you for all your help," I said.

Alex shrugged and smiled. "That's what brother's do. We stand by each other, right?"

"Right," I said.

Aunt Perrine was nowhere to be found when we returned. She had left dinner out for us on the table, but we couldn't find her.

"Look," Alex said and he pointed upward to Eleanor's window. It was lit. "She could be up there."

I followed Alex's lead and together we walked up the long dark stairs to Eleanor's little room. We stumbled a little and bumped into each other. We felt our way up through the darkness until we could peek around the corner and see into Eleanor's room.

The room looked like it had looked in Eleanor's vision. It was pretty and warm. Eleanor was sitting on her bed holding a stuffed bear and Aunt Perrine was sitting next to her. But it wasn't our Aunt Perrine. She had Aunt Perrine's eyes and Aunt Perrine's face, but in the prism of that room, Aunt Perrine was young. She was young and Eleanor was her daughter, her baby girl, and that is why Eleanor had never stopped waiting for her mother. Her mother had never died. Aunt Perrine held Eleanor in her arms and sang to her, songs so sweet they could have put a dragon to sleep.

I pushed my finger to my lips and Alex saw that we should leave. The two of us crept quietly back down the stairs and across the courtyard. We showered and ate our dinner, when we were done, we went into the living room. Aunt Perrine was sitting by the lamp, knitting. She was wearing her usual layer of sweaters and knitted hats. She was old again.

We went and sat down next to her. She didn't stop her knitting or look up at us. She only asked the simple question.

"So? What did you learn?" she asked.

I hesitated and looked at Alex. "I learned a lot," I said. "I learned that trolls can be kinder than people and that people can be more dangerous than zombies. I learned that trolls love the earth and their families, but mostly I learned that I couldn't have learned anything without Alex and that I can't be a monster hunter unless my brother is one too. So I guess you'll have to find another protégé, because I can't leave Alex behind."

Alex smiled when I said that and scooted a little closer to me. I looked at Aunt Perrine defiantly, thinking that she would say no. There could be only one monster hunter. That was the way it had always been. I expected her to be mad or at least disappointed.

"Good," she said. "You are a smart boy and both of you will be good 'elps to me. Tomorrow we wake up early and you will learn French and in zee evening, if you work 'ard, I will show you zee book."

"What do you mean?" I asked.

"I mean you will both learn from me and you will both take over when I am gone," she said.

"But...I thought there could only be one monster hunter," I said.

"Why would you zink zat?" Aunt Perrine asked.

"Eleanor said that there could be only one," I said.

"Just because there 'as always been one does not mean we cannot change. You two need each other. You vill be better together," Aunt Perrine said.

"Thank you," Alex and I said together.

That night Aunt Perrine popped popcorn and we all sat on her old couch and watched movies. We were an odd family. Uno, Roger, Eleanor, Alex, Aunt Perrine, and I, didn't look anything like a family should, but as we sat on the couch laughing I knew it was more important to feel like a family than to look like one. Alex sat by Aunt Perrine and she put her arm around him and I sat by Alex.

The sun set and the world was quiet. Alex and I had come home.

OUR STREET
BOOKS

Our Street Books for children of all ages, deliver a potent mix of
fantastic, rip-roaring adventure and fantasy stories to excite the
imagination; spiritual fiction to help the mind and the heart
grow; humorous stories to make the funny bone grow; historical
tales to evolve interest; and all manner of subjects that stretch
imagination, grab attention, inform, inspire and keep the pages
turning. Our subjects include Non-fiction and Fiction, Fantasy
and Science Fiction, Religious, Spiritual, Historical, Adventure,
Social Issues, Humour, Folk Tales and more.